THE SINGING G

To dear Janice ...
With love,
Vivienne
January 2016

THE SINGING GIRL

GIRL

VIVIENNE WOOLF

GAINSBOROUGH HOUSE PRESS
LONDON • PORTLAND, OR

First published in 2015 by Gainsborough House Press

Copyright © 2015 Vivienne Woolf

British Library Cataloguing in Publication Data

978 1 909719 04 0 (cloth)
978 1 909719 05 7 (paper)
978 1 909719 06 4 (kindle)
978 1 909719 07 1 (ebook)

Library of Congress Cataloging in Publication Data

Printed by CMP (UK) Ltd, Poole, Dorset

CONTENTS

THE SINGING GIRL

'To know nothing about yourself it to be constantly in danger of nothingness; these voids of non-being over which a man walks the tightrope of his life.' Athol Fugard.

PREFACE

CHOPPED HERRING

● ● ● ● ● ● ● ● ● ● ● ● ● ● ● ●

Combine four jars of pickled herring (skinned) in a mincer with crushed rich tea biscuits (about half a packet), 4 peeled granny smith apples and a medium onion. Decorate with grated strips of alternating white and yellow boiled egg.

● ● ● ● ● ● ● ● ● ● ● ● ● ● ● ●

A life is not complete till it has ended. But you don't need to know how a person lived to know how he will die because the one doesn't lead directly to the other.

And the way we know people when we are children is different from who they are. You need to live beyond a child's comprehension to understand.

However you interpret this according to Jewish custom, Eve died alone. Her daughter, Alice, kept a bedside vigil – cleaning and tending to her mother's face because she did not know what else to do - but Eve chose a private moment to go. Alice liked to think that her mother's solitary exit was the bravest act of her life. Alice liked to think that, in making this choice, her mother loved her enough to protect her.

Eve was fragile as a foxglove. As yesterday's certainties turn into today's conundrums, Alice wonders whether she knows anything about anybody – especially her mother.

The sadness began on the day of Eve's husband, Oscar's funeral (when the sun shone so brightly it was impossible to keep your eyes open). The rabbi made small cuts in the family's clothing and everyone present picked up the spade and dropped earth on to the lid of Oscar's coffin – as is the tradition. Although Oscar seldom attended synagogue, the rabbi said he was a man who lived his Judaism every day of his life.

Oscar promised he would live for ever but life does not always work out as planned.

Eve stood to one side, watching all this and greeting the assembled family as a hostess might at a party. She asked Alice where they were.

'We are at dad's funeral. Dad has gone to the darkness,' said Alice.

'Thank you so much for coming over. You must join us for tea,' Eve addressed the mourners.

Eve's admiration for Oscar never withered and all her life she tried to shore up against darkness rather than risk letting it in. Her own journey into darkness began on the day of Oscar's funeral. (This made perfect sense, in a way, for Eve was the wife of a physician and Oscar was her light).

After Oscar's funeral Eve asked to be taken home - thinking of her darkness. 'Home' was the sense of who she was and, if Eve had ever grasped this, it was beginning to slip away.

Albert, the cleaner, was a magician – in his way – and as strangely transparent as the air. He left the village of his birth to work in Johannesburg, city of goldmines because he could not take things any longer and the story which follows ends with him.

Albert explained to Eve and Alice that the painters in heaven mix the soil of Africa with the blackness of hell to make darkness.

Albert said, 'all dead people float on their backs through all the tears shed over them and above all the trees of the world to journey up to heaven.'

Albert said, 'if no vigil is kept for a dead body or prayers said for the departed, his or her soul might return among the living to disrupt or cause harm. '

PROLOGUE

PICKLED OX TONGUE

· · · · · · · · · · · · · · · · · ·

Cook tongue for half an hour. Throw away the water. Put an onion, two carrots, peppercorns, bay leaves and two cloves of garlic into the pot. Boil until soft (can take up to 5 hours). Skin tongue before serving.

· · · · · · · · · · · · · · · · · ·

In 1967 Oscar, Eve and Alice, their daughter, lived in Johannesburg in a white house built on a street corner in a 'whites only' suburb. Alice was protected from the world outside by the hum of housework and the silver oak and fir trees in the garden whose branches curved upwards as if in prayer.

(Building the white house was quite an undertaking. Apart from anything else, it was necessary for it to have a porticoed front entrance, swimming pool, upstairs bedrooms filled with light and downstairs rooms opening on to the lawn).

The street had a row of jacaranda trees assembled down each side of it and all the houses in it were made of brick. Most of the houses were two stories high but they were not all the same. Some had a fruit tree or two, some had grapevines, some had fish ponds, some double garages, some had flat roofs, some sloping, some had thatched roofs and mock Tudor beams. All had lawns mown so flat you could eat off them.

Oscar and Eve were more comfortably exiles in this suburb than anywhere else - and you realised they lived in a white suburb because there was no-one about to be seen.

The white house was both central and secluded and stood on a road which led from the northern suburbs to the goldmines. Like so many buildings of its kind the house was cold out of the sun and set back sufficiently that you could see only its chimneys from the road. Once inside, you could not hear the noise of traffic.

The house was famous for its garden. There were two splendid palm trees which stood by the swimming pool and flowers grew on the lawn, up trellises on walls, in circles under trees, in rectangular beds, in sinuous beds and in terracotta tubs dotted all over a veranda which extended out between rose beds.

The doorbell was a chime and you had to listen to a bar of Fur Elise before you could be let in.

Once inside, you saw charming interiors bathed in light and people gathered together in bizarre and dreamlike ways, chatting, reading, cleaning or cooking – even if there was nothing special about all this.

You saw watercolour landscapes, 'The Night Watch' painted by a local artist, standing lamps with fringed lampshades, flowers, clocks, mirrors, cushions, a piano kept open and in tune, darkly varnished floorboards covered in beautiful faded rugs (laid in straight lines), net curtains with oak leaves and berries on them and the sun bouncing off the edges of beautiful objects like sherry and brandy glasses and matching china cups and plates. You saw crocheted doilies and antimacassars but there were no television sets – not in Johannesburg – not at this time.

Everything looked as if it had been in place centuries before and there was so much stuff going on in the rooms, there was seldom any need for anyone to leave them.

Oscar married Eve in the same year that Nelson Mandela married his second wife, Winnie and they began life in a hotel on a road which later became a motorway. (Because a constant stream of people flowed up and down the road in cars and coaches, the first word Alice uttered was 'boo' for bus).

Everything about Oscar was thoughtful and modest.

Oscar fought in the British army during the Second World War and he never tired of telling his family that he had swum, fully clothed, from the beaches of Dunkirk to a British destroyer which delivered him to the white cliffs of Dover and safety.

Monday to Friday, he put on a neat white jacket over his suit and worked in a downtown hospital. (Oscar could see both the zoo and the goldmines if he hung out of the windows far enough - seeking 'distance and perspective' - and peered out to his right. An angry patient once threw an ashtray at Oscar and as it sailed past his head in the direction of the goldmines, Oscar found proof – if proof beyond Dunkirk were needed – that the forces of destiny were working to spare his life).

Oscar had soft grey eyes which seemed to say 'sorry' (because they knew the world) and he walked on tiptoe – a habit he acquired in hospitals. At weekends, he gardened with an urgent desire to clear his mind and as if nothing else mattered.

When Oscar gardened, he pushed the helmet he had worn as a soldier to the back of his neck so its rim could shield its dappled pinkness. Oscar clung to his helmet like you might anything left you by a loving grandparent or departed friend because the helmet absorbed his wartime memories and secured the past in his head.

In this family (so lost to each other or spread across continents) things were important – even if people tried to live their lives as if they were not.

Memories of loved ones were preserved in things, things had histories and stories to tell and when people were estranged from things, nothing seemed to work out.

Eve's mother's wedding ring reminded her that when life was bad for her it was never as bad as it could be. A green leather bound photograph album, a pearl necklace with a garnet clasp, a dinner service (with its hopes, intentions and its rim of green leaves) bought 'for best' and never used, a vase made in Bohemia, a brass camel which, it was said, once belonged to T.E. Lawrence, a much discussed samovar (who acquired it? and how was it used?), table cloths embroidered with flower baskets and kittens and Russian silver candlesticks were positioned by Eve in planned combinations of colour and size.

Eve was a planner. She planned out her life in exquisite detail and, sometimes, in daydreams so vivid she often forgot where the boundaries lay between the life she had and the life she planned.

Eve said, 'there is no problem so great that planning can't solve' and her time spent planning so satisfied her that when she did act on her plans, she often found she had lost 'the moment'.

'Don't do it that way, Beauty. This is the way,' Eve, the planner, called out to Beauty, the cook, who, feather duster in hand, prepared to arrange ornaments in patterns of her own.

Eve ran her house like a soldier and, together with Beauty and Albert the cleaner, most days passed smoothly and sunnily.

Although Eve was thankful for the quiet intensity of her life with Oscar (shaped and shifted by the seasons and the journeying of the sun), it was not difficult to upset the proportions of Eve's world.

There were days when Eve looked into the mirror for answers to questions of who she was. And there were days when Eve's thoughts so thumped around in her head they drove her to busy-ness; now cleaning silver, now arranging flowers, now repositioning furniture, now worrying about this and that and now protecting her husband from she knew not what – as if physical exertion could turn feelings into words.

Eve's struggle with her country's 'situation' was the same as anyone else's and she said, 'We need someone somewhere to change all this - if possible. Someone MUST step forward.'

(Eve did play a small part in shifting things by standing at the back of a group of women waving photographs of Nelson Mandela and crying out against injustice until the announcement came 'we are about to spray you with pepper spray again.'

It has to be said that some of the group were there simply because of personal grievances and older pains but this does not make their presence at the gathering any less meaningful).

The thought of this walk-on part in history brought Eve comfort. In fact, there should be an orchestra playing in the back of her mind to accompany the thought

'Yes,' Eve smiled to herself, 'there should be background music.'

When people talked of Eve, they always mentioned her appearance for Eve was a beauty with green eyes and wavy red hair.

On days when Eve felt misunderstood, insubstantial and wondered if she was going mad, she stood by her bedroom window and stared across to the golf course hoping that its yellow and brown patterns might settle her.

When the golf course brought the special gift of Gary Player, she gathered up her unsuspecting daughter, dressed formally (as if she were judging the competition), to watch the great man swing his club.

Alice did not know herself.

'Left for too long - or unexplored, this state of affairs might become dangerous,' said one of Eve's friends seated beside her on a bench under jacarandas whose heads bent together like giggling school girls.

Oscar was not a golfer and he did not have the anger to enjoy protesting, but he was a big father with big hands and a big life.

Every morning at eight he walked into the middle of the traffic to stop its flow with his best military salute so that his blushing daughter, wearing her maroon blazer with a protea emblazoned on its pocket, could make her way across to her school. (Oscar always left the house as if he were dressed in army uniform and about to cross the English Channel -and not just walk down the road with Alice. He asked Eve to 'wish him luck' then marched out and raised his hand for his daughter's crossing even when there were no cars on the road).

'You know your teacher's hands begin at her elbows,' said Eve one day when talking to Alice about overcoming adversity.

'That does not prevent her standing in front of the school choir conducting "Abide with Me".'

Oscar did not win a Nobel Prize or discover any cures, but he was not able to stop himself feeling empathy and had the privilege of easing the pain in some ordinary lives.

Oscar wanted Alice to be connected to his childhood so he told his daughter stories all rooted in the past.

He spoke of soldiers and synagogues, of heroism and heartache, of territory and tradition, of mothers, miracles and mourning, of Dunkirk and duty and, at night, held up his big hands to the light so they could make shadow puppets which danced on her bedroom wall.

Around this time, there were heroes in South Africa. People were defined by their political beliefs and some were dying for the colour of their skins.

Alice was not one of them.

Instead, her life was divided into slices of her mother's creating like a big white sponge cake served on a plate.

Alice knew the loneliness which children whose families have known 'situations' feel, and she hoped her parents had come to the land of blue sky so people could take away their sadness.

Alice believed there was a whoosh of fairies surrounding her family in a haze of pink and gold so she buried eggs in the lawn for them to eat and stamped grapes from the vine bound round the pergola to make wine for them to drink.

Alice preferred the view of the world from the top of a tree or the bottom of a swimming pool and she pushed the garden bench across the lawn - heaving now one side then the other - until it became either ladder or diving board. (The moving between tree and pool was part of the game and all was performed before an imagined audience of insects and animals who gathered for the spectacle).

There was no suggestion of the changes which would overturn the country at the end of the century; no hint of what was to come. For now, the city's destiny was whispered in the 'keep out' and 'keep off' and 'whites only' signs on the gates of public building and the silent queues of homesick black workers standing at bus-stops outside them. Centre of industry though this mining city was, Johannesburg's currency was fear.

The seasons rolled together from more to less sunshine, and almost imperceptibly.

But there were summers when people said 'the weather is crazy' and dashed for shelter. There were summers when flash floods, hailstones and (deadly accurate) lightning drove swimmers from pools, gossipers from telephones (for fear of electrocution) and walkers into shops. There were winters when the skies were blacker, stars brighter and the earth drier. And there were winters when the cold which descended drove night watchmen to their braziers in huddles and sleepers to bed wearing scarves and socks.

In a land where black was black and white was white, Oscar showed his daughter the grey, the orange, the yellow, the green and how not to be afraid of colour.

He taught his daughter to say 'Agapanthus', 'Strelizia' and 'physician' long before she could add or read and he said life was easier if you believed in God.

'There's god,' Alice decided as Oscar emerged, shears in hand, from the potting shed or rose up from planting bulbs or spraying weeds with his hands resting on the base of his spine.

Apartheid belonged to everyone but Oscar had a particular story attached to him.

To understand Oscar, you have to go away from Johannesburg with its shopping malls and mansions and its miles of golden grassland.

You have to go back to Oscar's childhood at the turn of the twentieth century in a village in Lithuania with a synagogue, market place and train station few people in Johannesburg know about. You have to visit the little wooden house where he lived with his grandparents in an area called the Pale of Settlement, marked out for Jews.

'What kind of place was your village?' asked Alice (in whose heart some of Oscar's village had settled like a visitor who should have left long ago).

Oscar lived a good deal of his life in the firmness of his past. His speech never lost the flavour of his village or the hold of his religious study. He spoke like the Bible and as if all fathers spoke this way.

'All I can be thankful for,' Oscar replied (as if addressing an adult), 'is that my village was too much of a backwater to suffer pogroms.

Our pavements were narrow planks which rested on wooden beams, our staple diet was potatoes, cream, cabbages and herrings (sold in barrels) and the market place was a bleak empty square except on Mondays when it filled with families, traders, thieves, drunkards, horses and carts.'

The Jews in Oscar's village lived for decades with their religious identity turned inwards. They knew next to nothing about the outside world unless there happened to be an epidemic.

'The comforting rays of tradition and the loving shield of our families protected us,' Oscar continued. 'I never heard the anxious talk or gossip which went on in back streets or on doorsteps and the whispers outside the synagogue (which was built like a fortress and where even the least religious could go for warmth – or to pray).

If Jews survived at all,' he said, pushing his helmet to the back of his head, 'it was through keeping silent and through God's grace. You didn't argue when you suspected everyone around you. You didn't argue when things were out of control.'

Oscar lived with his parents and brother in his grandparents' house and inherited his grandfather's grey eyes and accepting smile. For all of his life Oscar could not separate sadness from the feel of his grandfather's hand and, for all of his life, his way of living included everything his grandfather taught him.

The grandparents' house had a hardware store at the back of it and was always white-washed and spotless. There was a central oven with a circular wooden seat built around it on which Oscar's grandfather sat out his days. (Oscar's great uncle had his home and store next door and the brothers shared a vegetable patch. They must have inherited their home and land from their father but because no-one could agree on the position of the dividing boundary, the brothers never spoke).

There is one surviving photograph of Oscar's grandparents. Oscar's short, stout grandmother – who seems to stare out at her South African family with disbelief – has her thinning hair elaborately combed and tied in a knot at her neck. When Oscar looks at her photograph it is like looking at a photograph of his own face.

Oscar's grandfather was blind from cataracts, silent and studious. He had a neat side parting and was always photographed standing behind his wife with his hands resting on her back. He told Oscar to choose life over suffering because it's the right thing to do.

The season in the photograph is winter because snow is falling behind a window – visible even in the black and white.

Oscar hated winter's barrenness. When the snows came, the women of the village glued paper into the gaps between window panes and frames to keep the cold out of their houses but it still managed to seep through the glass.

Because the water in their own well froze over, Oscar led his grandfather by the hand to the well in the marketplace where they broke up the ice on the surface and carried the water home in buckets hung on sticks from their shoulders. (Few words passed between man and boy but the snow squeaked under their shoes as they walked and they could only wonder about who was watching or listening out for them from behind walls or from inside the church).

How could Alice understand Oscar's story of the people of faith in their black coats and hats who 'rustled through the marketplace like leaves in the wind, not in fear or shame - but with purpose'?

How could Alice understand Oscar when he said that he and his grandfather were 'propelled through the streets by nothing more than the tug of self-preservation'?

And how could Oscar tell his daughter that any protests against the tsar were crushed by cavalry charges with open sabres?

Nearly two million Jews left the Pale of Settlement for other countries at the start of the twentieth century, turning far-flung outposts in Africa, America and elsewhere into little pieces of Russia.

If you visit Oscar's village, you will not see the synagogue. It was dismantled – like holiness escaping.

Oscar's little house was razed to the ground by one of the many indoor fires his grandfather tried to extinguish with curtains wrenched from their poles or it may have been torn piece by piece by villagers wanting material for their own homes.

If you ask, people will tell you different things.

Some will say that the stone on the mound of earth in the cemetery marks the battle the brave Jews of the village fought on behalf of the Russians. Others will say that the stone marks the mass grave of the unsuspecting dead.

Some will say that Jews had stalls in the marketplace because they were shrewd merchants, others, that Jews were forced to trade because they could not own land. What all will say is that of the several thousand Jews living in the village at the turn of the twentieth century, none remain.

When Oscar turned eight, his father (like so many men before him – and some no more than teenagers) left his family in Lithuania hoping to seek the fortune he would never make in Johannesburg.

'We live with many lies,' he explained, 'but we can't talk about them. We live with many lies, but we are planning our escape.'

Oscar's mother, who would have given anything to be living in the future, waited for her husband - as all brides and wives in her position waited - and carried on with her domestic life.

But the villagers were not surprised when the family - mother and sons - set sail for Africa on a journey in search of something none of them understood, tempted away by the sunshine caught in a box of oranges sent to them from Africa.

Oscar never saw his grandparents again.

They were meant to follow but died instead on an exodus forced by the Russians in the face of the advancing German army. As they were nowhere near a cemetery, they were buried at the side of a road.

Oscar was haunted by his memories.

He never forgot the market place and the drunken stall holders chasing each other over rooftops with sticks and knives at the close of trading.

He never forgot the synagogue with its high up windows, fire under the pulpit and the sounds of rams' horns being blown into the air.

And he never forgot the train station, last sight of the village for so many people seeking a living or fleeing harm.

While he often wondered how far back he would have to move the sun to see his grandparents' house again, Oscar saw his grandfather's features every time people revealed to him the secrets in their sorrow or entrusted him to mend their pain.

Oscar's grandparents stayed with him as a place of belonging and greatness and while Oscar tried to live his life in the sunshine as if they meant nothing, he turned to his grandparents whenever he felt stranded in the present or whenever he said his prayers.

(Much later - in the future - Oscar was to be the face behind the building of the Johannesburg Jewish Aged Home. Above the front door are inscribed the words from his grandfather's favourite, Psalm 71: 'Do not cast me out in the time of old age. Do not forsake me when my strength is failing').

In this story the sun is a character.

The sun folded around bodies and caressed landscapes.

The sun was as much a part of every life in this story as the imprint it leaves behind the eyes when it has been stared at for too long.

The sun guided every decision and the sun was the magnet which drew people from snow-bound countries, families and familiar prayers to places so foreign, travellers wondered if they were dreaming.

When Oscar was reunited with him, his father had a rug spread over his knees and hands and all Oscar could see was his face.

He had learnt to speak English and said 'my sun began to shine only in Africa.' He lived with other immigrants in a house where the front door was never locked and flowers grew in unexpected places – like on the roof. The light on the trees outside his house (growing so close they touched the glass) threw dappled patterns on to him, making him look multi-coloured, fractured and foreign.

It was difficult to know what exactly had changed about him but Oscar's father spoke slowly now as if he were searching for a new self and in a whisper as if he were afraid to disturb himself in his new tongue.

He had been faithful. His wife was the only person he was close to and would look after and he carried on being faithful to her after she was gone. He still had the air of a man who thought deeply and from the moment Oscar saw him again, he knew he would take care of him until he died.

Young Oscar stood before him, cap in hand, small, puzzled and dishevelled from the train journey he, his mother and brother had taken across the Karoo Desert (which Oscar mistook for the Sinai).

'Ah! The sun,' Oscar explained to Alice in his Biblical tone. 'We went straight from our boat to a train on the dockside and travelled over vast expanse of desert land, rusty and dry, to Johannesburg. I knew of the Sinai desert from the narrative of the people of Israel's forty years' wandering. We could no more live without our father than he, us and here were the three of us, my mother, brother and I, chugging along through this land of the sun to regain our lost father. It was expected of us that we leave an environment and adapt to a completely different one. This was a tale, writ small, of our own Jewish wandering.'

Oscar's brother was a harpist who studied Sanskrit (a language akin to Lithuanian) and lived on the edge of life. He was rarely mentioned in the family and did not stay long in Johannesburg. Because this is a story about real life, he will make no more impact on it than a grey shadow caught tiptoeing across the words before it is chased away by bright colours and the force of the African sun.

For all of his life Oscar was pinned down by sadness because he had not seen his brother more. He said, 'My brother went to live in the north of England where he died, young, alone and forgotten by most – except by me.'

Despite the insistent pull of his instinct to protect his daughter from sadness, Oscar could not stop himself talking about his brother and about loss, yearning and love which might have been - any more than he could speak English without a foreign accent. When his brother died, Oscar told Alice of the invisible bonds between brother and brother and of those between the living and the dead.

He said, 'you can travel the world in search of someone only to find he lives in your heart.

What can I tell you about my brother, Alice? What is there to say?

In the end all we want is someone to yearn for us when they come to bury us in the ground.'

Because Alice's mind was full of dark mysteries and unanswered questions, she was busy elsewhere, imagining herself to be a leaf whirling through clouds to the sounds of harp music, seeking her lost uncle.

Albert, the cleaner, told himself stories. In one version of his story, he started life in a marsh and left it with a giraffe by his side as a kind of animal-god protector. (Had Albert been a giraffe once? Not clear). In another version, his giraffe protector led him away from his wife to the white suburbs of Johannesburg and in the version of the story he liked best, he earned sufficient money in the city to return to his wife (no need now for the giraffe) and take up where he had left off.

Jack, the gardener, thought Albert came out at night (long after other people arrived home from the activities the city demanded of them) and flew to the tops of the fruit trees to throw down the fruit Jack gathered up from the grass.

(Oscar just wondered if Albert was drugged and whether he smoked the dagga which Jack grew on the compost heap).

Albert told Alice that dead peoples' souls are caught in trees as they rise up to heaven and are pecked at by birds if people failed to say their prayers on earth.

Albert told Alice that a little of your soul lives within you and the rest lives in the sky. Albert told Alice that if you ask for your lost brother – or mother, father or sister - and then remain patient, the piece of your soul in the sky which knows your longing will one day drip an answer back to you.

'When you are looking for your brother, mother, father or sister, you see them in every rainbow, in the faces of lizards sunning themselves and in the rush of birds seeking light,' said Albert.

Oscar's mother died five years after her arrival in South Africa and a few months before Oscar's bar mitzvah.

Oscar did not know his mother was dead when he went walking that morning, lured outdoors by swimming pool skies. Because he did not know his mother would die that morning, Oscar was out in grasslands miles from home when they came to fetch him with the news.

Oscar did not talk about his mother for he found her remote and restless and did not remember sitting on her lap or being read to (even if he remembered trying to hold her when she cried).

For years after her passing Oscar could not understand his spiritual emptiness or others' lack of grasp of his point of view. Her death left Oscar with a fear (he could not explain) of making people cry and he wished for the power to stretch his arm into his past and change everything.

Four decades later, when Alice was born, a play of sunlight on her face threw up a hazy maternal memory for her father so Alice was named after his mother, Aleeza.

Alice loved sunshine, especially winter sunshine. She could sit on the garden bench in the comforting warmth of the winter sun, simply, without having to undress and jump about as she did in summer when the sun shone with such intensity, her pink skin burned beetroot.

Alice loved days when the only moving thing was the dust hanging in shafts of sunshine.

And she loved winter sunsets when smoke rising from coal fires and bonfires streaked the orange sky purple and made the windows of the white house look like funny little glass eyes.

Eve preferred to see the heat (which made rainbows on her dressing table mirror and could stop you in your tracks) than feel it. Her skin was untouched by the sun and as soft as jacaranda flowers.

On sunny summer afternoons she closed the blinds against the sun's glare and went to sleep till the air cooled, the crickets calmed down and Albert called out to say that the sun had begun its downward climb.

(Beauty went into the sunshine to hang clothes on the line. She had no interest in the sun beyond its value in showing up dust. She did so much living and working in the sun, she never thought of sitting in it).

Eve worried about money – going over and over in her mind amounts received and amounts due and, as there are no precise feelings in anyone, she was a lady of contradictions; embracing and rejecting, uncertain and insightful, conforming and unconventional. Eve looked both frail and robust at the same time like a rose growing on a thorny stem.

When Eve was alone, she shut her eyes and tried to remember her parents, but no specific pose or expression or tone of voice ever came to mind.

It was quite common for Eve's friends, who did not have wanderers in their heritage but, instead, gatherers of land and wealth – and who were always sure they were right – to smile at the same time as saying something unkind.

They asked Eve if 'her people' were still in Lithuania.

When Eve asked them questions of her own like, 'What will you do tomorrow?' they answered, 'Oh, you know – shopping.'

Apart from the people who lived in tune with the unspoken prejudice of the time and place (talking about those you couldn't 'trust with your silver' or to 'turn up at the right time'), Eve believed most people were nice when you got to know them and that most things in the world deserved praise but she feared she had lost the taste for shopping malls and traffic jams. Netball was the only sport Eve cared for – she had felt so free releasing the ball into the air. And her talent for the game had been noticed – but not enough to allow her to hang on to it all through her life.

Eve was drawn to different parts of her house depending on how the light touched the furniture and felt that there were rooms which had taken on her personality in a most pleasing way. (It has to be said that there were times when Eve felt an air of superiority come creeping up on her but this took her by surprise and she suppressed it).

Eve knew when cracks appeared in the surface of things - when patterns shifted or life did not work out as planned. When she asked herself the question, 'Why am I here?' and the answer didn't come, she settled into a pretend self and made do.

Because his peers (who were more of the world and cannier than he) did not know what to make of Albert, they left him alone. And because certain people made him gloomy, anyway, Albert told his stories to the moon which turned the garden silver (as if it had nothing to do with real life), tilting his head back in order to catch the light.

In Albert's stories, it was not enough that zebras had stripes or giraffes, long necks.

In Albert's stories, striped zebras kicked back and drank cocktails, alligators carried handbags, baboons dined off china plates and bad leopards lost their spots.

Alice wondered, 'was it Albert who turned eggs into fairies and silkworms into moths?'

Albert could not vote and he did not protest. He did not go to clandestine meetings to talk of freedom in basement hideouts and had never met, listened to or worked with Nelson Mandela. But Albert considered himself 'a bit of a storyteller' and his stories (which always had a moral) came from a time when animals still spoke to people.

'Be sure to respect your ancestors for they may induce sickness in the living to secure their companionship in the land of spirits' or

'When you discover what you are seeking, you had better prepare yourself to lose it again' or

'Do not crane your neck into other peoples' business or you risk ending up with their curses instead of their blessings' or

'Love waits for wounds to heal' or

'You cannot spend your life running away from your destiny. If your fate finds you hiding under your bed, it will send a snake there to bite you' or

'If you smile with the same face as you have when a snake bites you, you had better work on your face' or

'A traveller wandered through twenty years of life in search of treasure. After many years and many adventures, he returned, empty handed, to the place where he started, his spirit broken in two. A friend ran out to greet him, shouting, crying, smiling, sun glinting off her neatly chipped teeth. She had found his treasure in a box beneath his bed.

You travel the world in search of something and find it in the space and place of your birth,' or

'Beware of idleness. Once upon a time all the animals were invited to a tail receiving ceremony. When they returned to their homes at the end of the ceremony, all were adorned with beautiful tails except the lazy rock rabbit. He had stayed behind to sleep and was left forever tail-less' or

'When we want something very much, it is only when we go beyond wanting it that we stand a chance of receiving it.'

Some say that when Prince Albert's grandson, Prince Christian Victor, died of malaria in South Africa during the Boer War, a letter signed by his grandfather (which he carried in his pocket) was found by a relative of Albert's. From that day on, the firstborn males in Albert's family were named after Queen Victoria's consort.

No-one knows the truth.

Albert was a slight man with a brisk walk and his body always looked as if his mind wanted to flee. His face was not handsome - till he smiled - and his eyes glittered as if they had a life of their own, changing colour with light, which they seemed to swallow; brown by day and yellow-green at night.

When people remember Albert, it is gentle, laughing Albert they remember. When he spoke, his voice trembled like a leaf in the wind but when he laughed, the sound he made was like so many jacaranda trees coming into flower or the scattering of birds at nightfall.

Albert always laughed at something (even if he couldn't exactly recall what) - his head held back, a flash of gold from a tooth at the back of his mouth and punch lines all over his face. When Albert laughed, others smiled.

Alice liked being wherever Albert spent his days. She loved Albert's hands - for they were big-jointed and calloused, while managing to be feather-like at the same time and seemed strangely out of alignment with the rest of his body. When Albert pointed out to Alice the unlikely patterns of the constellations, Alice thought his hands switched on the stars.

Albert told Alice his stories and when he did, his hands fluttered above his head like pigeon's wings. Like his voice, his hands struggled to be still.

(Beauty was less receptive. When Albert spoke to her of cats and constellations, she wanted him to shut up so she could be alone).

Albert wore dark clothes and red trainers, which he polished till they shone and he played penny whistle tunes which the sky carried around the city.

When the buckets and brooms were packed away, dishes dried for the day, the garden swam with moonlight and the trees came out to shimmy their silver branches, something uncoiled inside Albert.

The story-teller guided the cleaner away from soapy water, polishes here and dusters there to the messy side of life where boundaries are blurred, sadness and uncertainty settle in cracks and Moonshine wipes daylight away.

Albert, the story-teller, pulled his woollen cap over his forehead, pushed his (rimless) glasses to the top of his nose and set words tumbling out of his heart and mouth so quickly he couldn't keep pace with them.

(Although Albert wore glasses, he did not have the proper face for them and they always slid away from where they should be. Because there wasn't much light in Albert's room, the electric light had to be on – even on a sunny day - and his glasses didn't seem to help him see at all. Albert dreamed of living the life of a man who had no need of glasses).

Separated as they were by the colour of their skins and the scope of their experience - and difficult as it is to imagine Albert's having a mother, Albert and Oscar shared an experience: Albert's mother died when he was thirteen.

When Oscar's mother died, he wrote to his aunt (who thought how strange it was that her sister died in a place she had never seen) to announce her passing.

He explained - in his particular way - that he, together with his father and brother, could not express their thoughts or feelings about their tragic loss because 'each lived in his own inner castle.'

Because Albert forgot where he came from, because time rearranges things and because he never thought of losing his mother because he didn't think about having her, Albert accepted his mother's passing.

Albert did not form a memory of his mother and soon stopped imagining her as a different person or her possible future life or any other children she might have.

Rather, he remembered his fear and loss.

'You are all alone, Albert,' said Eve one day. 'You are looking for your lost mother.'

'Thank you - but I am not,' Albert replied. 'Mother made it to forty-five and her gift to me was the stories I tell which help me carry on.'

Not for Albert the luxury of grief.

(When his wife died, Albert's father let his son go even if it meant never seeing him again. He tried his best to make his son see that it was so much better to have money than be poor and explained that all he had in the world was a field filled with dead brown grass and the crates of mealies and peaches he sold on the streets each week.

'Get on. Get on with your life,' he told his son, 'and leave me be with mine. Only, be sure to fix the place of your birth in your heart so you can return to it when dark times come knocking.')

Oscar and Albert recognised in each other a mutual brokenness and, because of this, they never wanted to share an experience again.

It was something of a coincidence that they ended up under the same roof, but a coincidence which confirmed Oscar's sense of predestination. Oscar remembered his mother as 'regal' or 'remote' but if Albert remembered his mother at all, it was of her lying dead. Albert struggled to remember, anyway, hoping that if he remembered anything, it would be his next step.

'What is my next step?' he often reflected or 'what will take me away?'

When Albert left his wife to seek his fortune, he asked himself, 'where do I go from here? What is my next step?' and 'what is it about me?'

(Albert wondered if there were correct answers to these questions and whether he was the one to answer the questions, anyway).

When Albert left his wife he simply imagined a life away from the village of his birth. When Albert left his wife, he was just a boy travelling to a city, trying to decide what to do.

(Albert never imagined he would work in a place where the grass was so green, the houses so clean and there were white people he could like).

When Albert left his wife every step of the journey away from her seemed improbable.

When Albert left his wife he wondered if not having a mother may have had something to do with what he did and how he felt.

When Albert left his wife he could not remember the colour of her eyes.

When Albert left his wife he wanted to say something to her but could not find the words. At least, he could not find words which would make any difference.

But love never dies.

From time to time visions of his wife crossed Albert's mind, entangling themselves in his head, piling up like a car crash and distracting him from the story he was telling or the cleaning task in hand.

When this happened, Albert went off with his arms outstretched, crying, 'My memory is inside me. I think of you because my entire life faces the wrong way except when I think of you. I may have forgotten what you said, but I remember the sound of your sadness.'

If his wife were there, at the end of the garden, she might reply, 'I think of you too. I keep vigil for you. The blanket I hold to me at night makes me feel close to you. But all this doesn't change a thing.'

(There was a woman at the end of the garden but she was just the strange middle-aged woman who leant over the wall and who saw ghosts in trees and houses. She walked around looking for the dog she had rescued from a swimming pool and would be happy to see again – even at the end of someone else's lead. She scurried away as Albert approached).

If Alice caught Albert walking off like this, she called out, 'Where are you, Albert?' (Alice found Albert unattainable and always felt excluded. Were Albert a song, he would always sound his sad notes out of Alice's earshot).

'Are you sad, Albert?' Alice asked when Albert returned to her.

Albert tore himself from thoughts of his wife. His love asked nothing of Alice.

'I'm not at all sad,' he replied.

(How could Alice know that that's what sad people always say?)

All Albert wanted to be was a man sitting alone on a bench, staring at no-one and happy about a life without much achievement. Albert asked for nothing else.

He did not want to be white, for example - or famous.

Did Albert feel well? Probably not. Tiredness crawled all over him.

Albert had a sense of how difficult things were going to be for Alice – with her puzzling presence in the world. He shook his head as if to clear it and knelt down beside the little white girl; his love for her as strong as the buzzing of a bee.

'Hello Miss Alice.'

(Because he made circles in the air when he spoke, he wafted his arms up to the moon perched on top of the jacarandas as if he were surprised to see so much light in the sky).

The thrill of regaining Albert's attention made Alice wish she could say something to amuse him but all she could do was sit back, hope he didn't say something too 'message like' and pretend she knew what he was talking about.

Then she shut her eyes so she could hold Albert's face in her head.

'Could we sit here for ever?' she asked.

'No,' Albert replied.

'What were you doing when my back was turned?' he asked.

'Just thinking,' said Alice.

1
OSCAR AND EVE

BEAUTY'S CHEESE SCONES

• • • • • • • • • • • • • • • •

Cup grated mature cheddar; cup flour; cup milk; pinch mustard; 2 heaped teaspoons baking powder.

Mix all ingredients together and place spoonsful of the mixture into greased patty pans, filling them only half way up. Bake for twenty minutes. Enjoy.

• • • • • • • • • • • • • • • •

Saturday, 9th December. (Jack is out in the garden cutting the midsummer grass).

Johannesburg is not a subtle city. Its stories are simple and its colours vivid. It began as a rough, disorganised, shabby place of little distinction - home to prostitutes, gangsters and the disaffected.

But it is 1967 and Johannesburg is going through a phase. (Its gated houses, sun burned patios, guarded suburban streets and gleaming shopping malls are no permanent expression of what the city could be. And people like Beauty and Albert, Eve and Oscar, so bound in time to their city, seem not to be possible any more).

It is 1967 and Eve has changed her hairstyle - her hair is blonder and more bouffant. She lives in this sprawling city, girdled on the southern fringe by mounds of greyish-white mine dumps. The flow of immigrants has swelled Johannesburg's population and, among them, Jews enjoy freedom previously denied them in the ghettoes of their birth.

When people talk of Johannesburg, they rarely mention its appearance, but six million trees grow here. And if you travel a mile or two from the city centre you will find yourself in open farmland.

'Johannesburg is so empty in places that when a murder pops up, no-one know about it,' says Eve.

Eve has a strange confidence in Johannesburg and likes it for its difficulties. She finds beauty in the dry brown of winter, in the lilac sky hanging down on you after a storm, in the musicians slouched on shady corners, the Saturday shoppers and the still suburban streets.

This story begins on a Saturday morning in summer when the sky's gift to the garden is a thin sliver of moon still visible in the blue. Two tall palm trees are reflected, trunks up, in the swimming pool.

Beauty doesn't know the names of many trees and she doesn't care about the differences between them but she has yet to see anything particularly South African about palm trees.

Albert knows trees.

Take the baobab. Albert says it looks as it does – with is spindly branches rising out of its fat trunk – because God gave the slothful hyena the task of planting it and he planted it upside down.

Albert says that trees grow their crowns in the image of their roots. Oak trees represent strength, tiny termites can cause the collapse of any tree and the acacia is the giraffe's favourite because his mouth and tongue are so tough he can't feel the prick of its long, sharp thorns.

The magnolia tree growing close to the white house has dark green leathery leaves which bang on the windows when the wind blows and if the purple flowers of the friendly jacaranda fall on your head, you will know good luck.

Eight year old Alice thinks all trees are for climbing. The syringa (with its purple flowers) has a branch she can crawl on to for a view of the garden and to survey the world she presides over with its blossoms and its bees.

Here she is, sitting on a stone mushroom in a rose bed, listening for the background clatter of insects you would never hear unless you stopped to think about it.

Being alone in a bed full of roses allows Alice to plan her escape.

If she sits long enough and wills it enough, the mushroom will fly her through the night skies to animals and palaces far away. (Although her planned flights are solo, Alice can't exclude her parents from her arrangements, so until the day comes when she leaves them behind for good, she flies with them in tow).

On the grass beside Alice is the knitted donkey which accompanies her on her travels and which her father bought at the fun fair where people with big sunburned faces stood around laughing.

Oscar does not have a big sunburned face but he bent over his daughter and handed her the knitted donkey saying (in his mysterious accent), 'here's a little donkey for you Alice,' and, softer now because he remembers having to brush the hair off his grandfather's cow to make his own toys, 'a little donkey.'

(Alice practises her spelling on the donkey. 'How do you spell "fluctuate", "seasonal", "brightness", "thoughtful"?'

Other than this, the donkey plays no part in this story. All Alice expects it to do - one way and another - is keep up. If it can't, Alice waits until it can).

To the outside world, Alice is a helpful girl who is going to make her parents' tribulations worthwhile.

In Alice's earliest memory, she and her father have their faces pressed against glass looking out on to a garden. Her father is wearing a grey suit and his eyes are shining. Alice is wearing a white organza dress and lace-up boots with ankle socks inside them. Her father is telling her a story about the fate of the wandering Jew.

'What a wonder it is that people, denied all kinds of freedom, had the courage to get where they went, leaving everything and turning their backs on everything they knew. But all works out - as it must - in the end,' said Oscar.

For now Alice is a shape seeking substance. She is waiting for life to begin. Alice knows neither herself nor her loneliness. She loves the garden because she finds treasure there and because, so far as she knows, she loves nothing else so much.

There is nothing very unusual about Alice's appearance. Eve says 'stay out of the sun,' but Alice's face is radiant with freckles and there is a quizzical expression etched around her earth coloured eyes. Her eyelashes stick out like sunbeams and she wears her hair, which is brown and red and gold (mark of her mother's family), plaited to her waist or hanging in a bush around her shoulders.

Child of her time, Alice stays in step; in step with the seasons and in step with her parents who stay in step with each other when they dance rumba, samba and foxtrot in their faded pink bedroom to 'Nowhere Man' and 'Love, Love Me Do'.

Alice is not like other girls.

She recognises individual birds and butterflies and falls in love with a green leaf, a star, a butterfly's wing. Alice knows that if you plant the right flowers the whole garden becomes a bird sanctuary or butterfly farm and that dragon flies hang motionless in the air even when their wings are flapping.

She loves secret things and, deep down, feels she is a princess, or a tiny creature from another planet speaking in a mysterious tongue which the clamour of the garden drowns out. When Alice sees her father's helmet supported by the back of his head and a faraway look in his eyes, she wonders if he comes down from heaven and whether it is quiet up there.

'Best left for future consideration,' her parents say (without explaining the feelings they attach to this plan) is the still, sad, unspoken realisation that Alice may have to move away from the white house - even if it means never coming back. And this plan hangs over the garden like a miserable packet of seeds which sometimes, unbidden and misunderstood, spills into Alice's soul.

For now, though, Alice is hopeful. She has a fairy tale in her head.

In Alice's head Oscar gardens without wearing his helmet because he has put his past to rest and, in Alice's head, Eve wipes away her 'hostess' smile, fills her mouth with grape jam and laughs a great big purple 'don't give a damn' laugh.

In Alice's head Beauty puts down her duster, leans against the piano and sings 'Summer Time' along with Miriam Makeba before exiting the white house with the words, 'then I'll spread my wings and I'll take to the sky.'

In the fairy tale in Alice's head, she will fly off, strong as the geese in the yard, across rivers and deserts with her parents resting on her wings.

Eve watches her daughter reflected three times in the mirrors on her dressing table. (Alice knows something about her mother without knowing exactly what because it is so long buried in silence. When Alice does remember, it is the story of her mother's mother which comes in to her mind).

Eve is anxious to save her daughter from she knows not what and busies herself thinking about how her daughter should be, how she should behave and whether she should wear a cardigan.

Eve still has a bit of energy and thinks, 'It's as much as I can do to hold our lives together – as much as I can do.'

There are times when Eve feels like jumping out of her bedroom window into the garden's shadows.

There are times when Eve sees (with surprising intuition) that her daughter might be weighed down by the same concerns she has worked so hard to subvert. And there are times when Eve feels compassion for the little girl so hard at work rearranging the world in her head.

Oscar – sixty-year old father of an eight year-old child - is planting roses called 'Boksburg Fantasia' and 'Beauty from Within'.

He is wearing his army helmet, his hands are mottled white and pink with vitiligo and his voice is soft and sad. Man of certain faith but uncertain country, Oscar passes his time assembling the sounds and sights of his childhood so he can piece them together to tell his stories. Oscar's accent is so full of mystery that visitors seeking the owner of the house believe him when he directs them indoors. If Oscar were a song, it would be about 'moving on' – 'moving on' and played on a guitar.

There are times when Oscar dreams of battles he has fought with glory.

Other times, he feels uncomfortable with himself as if he were his own guest who had over-stayed his welcome.

Not for the first time Oscar thinks that his world built with bricks fired by the oppressed is a world built to crumble. Now, he scatters and sows, waters and weeds, picks and prunes with black Jack, the gardener, by his side, a counterpoint to his whiteness and moving in rhythm.

Jack is slow from Moonshine and his eyes are rheumy. He is civilian batman to Oscar and Oscar is Jack's reason for living.

'Do you have stories about the dead people?' Alice asks her father, swinging her legs.

(Alice's life is full of stories. She loves her father's stories but doesn't know what to do about them. She often wonders if he is the guardian of important secrets. Her father just fears that all this talk of dead people is an invasion of their personal sanctity).

Oscar thinks of the place of his birth where there are lots of dead people buried together in a mound marked, simply, with one stone. Eve had a friend called Lea who died of an illness called the 'c word' and bequeathed Alice the brass dog brooch she is wearing and a teapot with the words 'we see things as we are not as they are' engraved on its spout. (When Eve told Alice about Lea's passing, Alice looked down at her own reflection in the glass top of her bedroom table hoping to find words of comfort for here was a moment between her and her mother, rare for its content of shared confidence, and Alice did not know what to say).

'I have a story from now,' says Oscar, trying to sound less like the Bible.

Oscar clears his throat, rises up from planting with his hands at the base of his spine and cuts up slices of watermelon for him and his daughter to share.

'No. I mean about dead people from before,' Alice insists.

Perhaps under different circumstances, Oscar might speak of his Lithuanian village. He might paint the grey of his childhood with washes of colour to comfort Alice. But here is Johannesburg with its orchards and its goldmines and its lines of migrant workers wrapped in coloured blankets seeking comfort in soft music.

Oscar and Alice play tennis on the lawn between the rose beds, using an upturned bench as the 'net'. The game is warm and slow but Oscar thwacks the ball so low and hard that Alice (whose size helps her squeeze between the thorns) rummages through bushes more than she returns shots. When his daughter does hit the ball, Oscar shouts, 'good shot' – but most of the time he shouts 'sorry!' At the end of the game, Oscar does not embrace his daughter but puts his hands on the top of her head and holds them there for a long time as if any movement would trigger the feelings he tries so hard to contain.

(Eve tells her friends, 'a tennis ball once strayed out of our garden into the hands of the man – you know the one - who walks around the neighbourhood with a cross on his back – for the sins of the world. He picked it up, scrutinized it as if it were an item of great significance then threw it back to us with a flick of the wrist which suggested skill he might have nurtured another time or place.'

Eve believes that life gives us signs we should take seriously so she says, 'This was significant,' then asks, 'but why?

If you stand here – just here - you can see my husband's solemn grasp of the racquet and Alice's bitten finger nails.')

Father and daughter cannot know this, but Oscar will live in this brave and struggling city long after Alice has left.

Oscar will die soon after Mandela's release from prison – as if he feels able to leave the world in better hands - and with no inconvenience to others, just as he has lived. He will be buried in Johannesburg near the memorial to the six million lost in the Holocaust.

Beauty will tell Alice that Oscar died in her arms and this will help Beauty face her own dark death which comes ten years after Oscar's because she refuses to take her pills.

Inside the house, Beauty feels her emptiness stretching out into the endless light.

(On days like this, the venetian blinds are half closed against the sun and send its rays out in stripes across the floors).

Albert says, 'you should enjoy your life, Beauty.'

Beauty says, 'that's true.'

Something or other always asks for Beauty's attention. Here she is, gliding past as if on wheels, dusting (just so) the keys of the baby grand bequeathed to Oscar by the patient who played 'Moonlight Sonata' on it every night before she went to bed and said Oscar was the only man she ever liked.

Now Beauty is dusting Eve and Oscar's wedding photograph in the silver frame – just so.

Beauty does not need to look at the photograph to know that Eve is a head taller than Oscar - and beautiful. Oscar's face looks full of light. Everything is austere in the black and white but, in life, Eve wore a tulle veil, clouds of ice-blue satin (which swished around her like a breeze through trees when she walked down the aisle) and carried yellow daffodils. Oscar wore a navy blue suit and had a red carnation pinned to his lapel.

(When Beauty dusts the photograph, she imagines she can hear Eve saying, 'Do it this way, Beauty' and she replies 'But I am.'

Much later on, this photograph will take people back to the time when Oscar smiled and Eve had ginger hair).

Beauty dusts a ladybird off the top of the frame – just so - before tickling the brass camel with the lucky hump given to Oscar by the patient whose parrot said 'bacon and eggs for breakfast' and 'why don't you say something?'

(Although she has never seen Arabian deserts, the brass camel always makes Eve think of nights full of promise and delight she imagines she could spend there).

The house is silent. It is so silent that Beauty's vacuuming disturbing, as it does, the light and the shadow across the floor, sounds as loud as the Stukas which flew over Dunkirk on the day Churchill named 'the miraculous day of deliverance.'

Oscar is not a military type, but battles and sinking ships are a constant backdrop to his life. Eve wonders why so many men view their military service as the defining event of their lives.

'It is a day in 1940,' says Oscar – coming up with a story. 'I am a lieutenant colonel in the British army. As the sun comes up the men are divided with orders to walk along the dunes to Dunkirk. Each man is for himself.'

As we near Dunkirk we see some dead bodies washed up on the sands and the odd German bomb explodes. In the entrance to a burning building, I see an officer peering ahead of him repeating the phrase, 'I am watching history in the making. I am watching history in the making.'

God knows if he survived.

At nightfall I try – and fail - to get on a boat and across to England. Ahead of me I see men making their way to a jetty whilst others are swimming out to boats of all descriptions waiting offshore. Some are drowning in front of me.

I stand through the night with hundreds of others waiting for dawn to break. Shortly after sunrise a British destroyer reaches us. I clamber onto it to the shouts of the men on board to hurry up as we are sitting ducks for the Stukas. I crawl into a corner of the ship and fall asleep until I am awakened by our arrival at Dover on 1st June at 9.30.'

Alice knows the story of the day of deliverance. She knows about the fishing boats, yachts and ferries which were sent from Britain to France.

Oscar says the story of his rescue from Dunkirk is a story about the forces of destiny working to save his life. Alice thinks about the soldiers who went to the bottom of the sea. She decides that her father's story is a fairy tale in which she can imagine herself starring and that somewhere in the garden, where the fir trees are scraggy and the sunlight plays on their branches, are the shadows of marching soldiers and the lap of waves on sand.

'Wars were different then,' Oscar concludes, putting a spoonful of Beauty's katorba jam (made from grapes which pop right out of their skins when squeezed) into his mouth before drinking his tea.

'There was right and there was wrong and you knew the difference between the two. You fought for your country and weren't unhinged by a fight which drags on for longer than you can bear.'

England was so dreary after the war Oscar thought he would die of cold and, as Dunkirk hadn't got him (God be thanked) he returned to live in South Africa, turning his back on the fog.

Because he never got over the cold winters of the war or the nights spent on the beaches of France, Oscar's lungs are bad. There are times when he coughs so much, he has to steady himself against trees or the garden wall (which leans so close to the pavement, the bougainvillea climbing up it cling on for dear life).

Today is Saturday – Oscar's day in the garden.

On weekdays Oscar works in the downtown hospital near the zoo where giraffe poke their heads above doors instead of baobab trees and elephants, who never forget the place of their birth, have lost the taste of a kill and the thrill of a sunset walk, trunk in tail.

Albert says, 'the elephant and the giraffe are in conflict: the elephant is older than most trees so has ruled them for a long time. The giraffe thinks trees belong to him because he struts above them.'

Albert is in his room, dreaming away his sadness.

When Albert dreams, his beard trembles with pleasure. (His good dreams don't keep him awake but when Albert has nightmares which go in a bad direction, he has to stop them by waking up).

Albert dreams he is a giraffe walking under a cloud which crosses the sun. He sees his mother's face calling to him from a cloud saying, 'sorry I haven't been in touch. See you again soon' and Albert feels unsettled and full of longing. (When Oscar dreams about his mother, Albert doesn't know about it; the men hide their dreams from each other).

Albert wonders, again, if he was a giraffe in a former life. He may have been.

Whoever Albert is and wherever Albert is, he thinks of the wife he left behind under the burning sky of the village of his birth. With a flash of nostalgia, he tastes the sourness of her breath and smells the baby porridge smell of her skin.

Albert misses her more deeply than anything he felt when they were together and he hears her voice in everything around him from birds' skyward sweep at sunset to the vain honking of horns in the morning traffic rush.

Albert's first experiences are bound to his wife just as much as she is the reason for his gambling and he hosts parties where people come to his room to gamble and drink his home made Moonshine. (Moonshine doesn't make Albert fall about or have fights. It helps him see the world. He is not afraid of drunks or of angry voices because he never sees himself going under).

There are nights when Albert dreams he is gambling with Eve and Oscar – people who, in real life, would not be in the same room as he. When he is woken from these dreams (by a breeze or a whisper or a wing), he finds himself in a lonely bed watching the moon rock from side to side.

If any woman shares Albert's bed these days, it is the woman who wears a green dress through which you can see her underwear and skin the colour of maltabella and whose hair is shaped in cornrow plaits piled high under a scarf.

(The woman in the green dress sometimes wears a green hat with a veil over her eyes.

She says she comes from Mogadishu – although she could be making this up. When she closes the garden gate behind her, her hair sticks out in strands from her up-do and hangs limp with sweat on her cheeks).

Eve sits in front of the (stinkwood) dressing table in her bedroom away from the air outside which is smoky from the fire on the compost heap. She spits on a black pad of mascara and dips the brush into the gloop.

The mirror on the table has two side wings and when she turns these inward to apply her make-up, she sees herself in triplicate with three reflections of the garden behind her, framing her faces like halos. Eve's faces in the glass are rainbow faces painted red like Fire Engine Lipstick, yellow, her box pleated skirt, blue, her coat with the pearl buttons, green, her summer hat – and violet, the colour of her bed jacket - which colour prevails over all.

The sky behind Eve is blue, pink and cloudless – same as the day she accepted Oscar's offer of marriage.

'I could no longer endure my loneliness,' said Oscar as he knelt before his beloved. 'By a wondrous turn of fate you came into my life to rescue me from despair. Here are we, two human beings, who waited long in the wings for this chance of happiness. May I offer you my hand?'

Eve was so surprised by Oscar's declaration of love, she felt as if she had swallowed a sunbeam.

Because she loved him and because no-one else spoke like this, she accepted his offer and they were married after only five weeks of courtship.

'The first year of my marriage was the happiest of my life,' Eve said – and, as the words came out of her mouth, she realised she was telling the truth.

Eve's mother had flame coloured hair – mark of the family – and was plucked out of her life by a matchmaker to marry her husband – just as her parents were chosen for each other and their parents before them in a snowy Polish village long, long ago.

(The story goes that Eve's mother was called 'the singing girl' but all stories about her – except those about her courage - seem to contain one untruth or another.

The singing girl kept her songs for her husband and sang so quietly, there were times when you could tell she was singing only because she had closed eyes.

One day, she was forced to sing before people who had the murder of Jews on their minds. After hearing her songs, and without remotely guessing what her truth might be, the people let her and her husband on their way.

A year later, Eve's parents found themselves travelling to a camp in a sealed cattle train under a watching moon. The singing girl jumped out of her wagon through a space between wooden slats and travelled alone from where she landed on the tracks to South Africa.

Because Eve's father lacked the courage to follow his wife, the singing girl never escaped the sense that she had set her husband free only to see him recaptured. She also never escaped the sense that her heart belonged to another world.

Eve knows all this because it is fact).

But because Eve no more talks about her mother than Alice talks about hers and because Eve skims the surface of the part of her life which can't be shared with her daughter, all she says, for now, is, 'One day, you will know.' When Alice asks for more, all Eve says is, 'There are some things you keep to yourself' and gives a shuddering movement before her silence.

Eve - with her red hair streaked with grey, liquid green eyes and deep eyelids, is often mistaken for someone who comes from the British Isles. She likes her looks and is cheered by her face in the mirror but she frets about her life of chores, routines, seasons and pleasantries and would like to be someone else.

Eve would like to be the postwoman in the brown trouser suit who cycles past the house, the waitress serving ice-cream floats at the drive-in cinema, a diver with tanks on her back scouring the sea bed for ship wrecks or a doctor suggesting, 'leave this to me.' These are the lives in Eve's head and, when no-one is about, she lives in them. Eve takes the lives out of her head and holds them before her on lazy summer mornings or on half lit winter afternoons when, moving from room to room to keep warm, she wonders at the gap between the woman she is and the professional netball player she might have been.

Half-light brings Eve comfort.

Eve started life in the half-light cast by her gifted older siblings. While they studied, she sat on the garden wall affecting an air of studiousness, wearing little else but, on her nose, a hairpin fashioned into spectacle frames, wondering at her life lived in half-light when her siblings lived in such a sunny blaze.

Eve stands by her bedroom window, watching the landscape change.

'There's a bird pecking away at the nectarines, a tree with flowers so white they are almost blue and Jack –there's Jack coming out of the shadows, carrying so much of the garden into the kitchen, it's like watching Birnam Wood march on Dunsinane Hill.'

(Eve remembers reading 'Macbeth' with her hairpin glasses on her nose. The glasses were the unwitting cause of a near death experience. Young Eve wandered into a field wearing her hairpin glasses and looked up to find herself surrounded by a group of interested bulls. One of the bulls dipped its horns, hoisted Eve up and threw her over a fence. As Eve lay on the ground she decided that the hairpins were an obstruction to her vision and that she would never wear them again).

Eve would like to be carefree and float through the garden, trailing her fingers through the flowers' bowing heads and admiring the many shades of mauve and yellow in the beds and the various blues of the shade. But the sun troubles her. There are times when (sitting beside Oscar on the lawn, taking tea) Eve has to leave the garden without finishing her drink and her cheese scone in order to lie down.

'Why shouldn't I?' she answers when Beauty asks why she takes to her bed while the sun is up, adding, 'I know you keep my secrets, Beauty.'

Eve is not the sort of person who thinks that because you iron your napkins you have a civilized attitude to life. Eve would like to tear away the string on packages with her teeth.

She would like to dance flamenco, stamp and strut through the streets wearing a red flounced skirt. Eve would like to flick her shoes, slick back her hair, stick a carnation in her mouth, flare her nostrils and clap her hands to the rhythm of 'Volare'.

'These days, who can tell who will be popular next year?' asks a friend.

Eve would like not to care.

On days when Eve plays bridge in the sunshine with ladies who sit with their cardigans draped over the backs of their chairs, Eve dresses in protective long sleeved blouse, wears sun block cream on her face and places herself in the shade cast by her parasol.

Eve is an extremely good bridge player but she often feels a sharp longing for her imagined world. She seeks –but finds no - understanding in the faces of her friends whose voices seem somehow to be related to their cardigans.

('The thought of my dancing,' muses Eve, housewife, when Eve, flamenco dancer, stomps into her head during a card game. 'The very thought of it.')

The bridge ladies' talk is either approving or disapproving and they know only people who are 'influential' - whose husbands go to work in suits with flowers in their lapels. They see films which are 'important' (they say shade is 'important': one of them once fell asleep in the sun and turned purple and hard as wood before she could be ushered indoors and given lemonade to drink) and play cards until the ice melts in their tea.

Eve is afraid the players will ask, 'Are you a Jew?' because being Jewish once meant she could not be the golden netball player she wanted to be – the one with the easy charm.

In Lithuania, many Jewish parents rushed their young children (who never knew if they were going into happiness or sadness) into marriage before the tsars could stop them. Oscar and Eve met in late middle age.

Grateful for the late and unexpected chance of happiness, Eve tries to be everything Oscar lacks. She fills vases with his garden; nasturtiums, strelitzia, zinnias, Michaelmas daisies, Shasta daisies, fuchsias, fat yellow sunflowers and predatory looking purple flowers with lime markings on their petals (called phalaenopsis) until the whole house is full of Eve and the scent of her flowers. (She instructs Beauty to place them on tables in descending order of size – just so).

Because he was born in the Pale of Settlement, Oscar thinks differently. (He has seen too much overturned to want more).

Oscar and Eve talk a great deal but come and go at different times and know when to leave each other alone.

Oscar strains to be South African (thinking, 'if you want to get anywhere in this country you have to be as mainstream as possible') and pins unfamiliar words like 'dumela' and 'unjani' and 'hoe gaan dit' to his bathroom mirror so he can call out the sounds they make while shaving and send them floating to Eve's feet.

Everybody knows about September 11th 2001. Few people know that Eve suffers when she can't be seen.

Eve's journey into darkness will begin on the day of Oscar's funeral. The World Trade Centre will crumble as her body is lowered into the ground and her burial will be mixed up with lots of blinking at newspapers and radios.

When people talk of Eve after her passing, it will be those who attach their emptiness to her so that 'Eve of 9/11' will fill a gap in their lives nothing else can. After that day, no-one in Johannesburg will talk of the 9/11 bombing without calling it 'Eve's story.'

Alice knows none of this. Her mother is her mother.

Alice is curious. She turns jacaranda pods into castanets, pops fuchsia buds open, squeezes the pock-marked shells of granadillas till black and orange rivers run down her arms and listens out for the crickets' twilight chirp. Alice knows that you put bugle lilies on each of your fingers – like witches' talons (as Albert showed her) to ward off evil spirits and the snake handlers at the zoo (standing bare-chested in the snake pit) told Alice that you treat snake bite poisoning with snake venom. (Albert said that you shed many lives in your journey through earth just as the snake sheds his skin).

But Alice does not ask her mother about her childhood, the school friends she never sees or whether her grandmother spoke of her country laid waste. (If Eve were to answer these questions, anyway, her whole life might blow up in her face).

The mother Alice knows lives in the make-up basket on the dressing table or in the wardrobe of brightly coloured dresses.

When no-one is looking, Alice creeps into the dark cool of her parents' bedroom to smell the musky sweetness of her mother's clothes, sniff at her lily of the valley scented eau de cologne and scrape and clop around in her high heels.

Here is Alice, caught in the full length mirror on the wardrobe door wearing ankle socks, her mother's shoes and a starched petticoat under her mother's skirt.

Because Eve is remote, Alice clings to her things.

Alice is not yet beautiful and there is something unsettling about her as if at any moment she might begin dancing in the flower beds or join the mix of insects, stirred up differently every day.

What kind of life is Alice preparing for?

She is not.

It never occurs to Alice that anything in her fragile world might change. She is simply convinced that her life is special and held in place by ties which can never be broken.

When the sun sets, Alice sits at the top of the stairs watching her parents waltz their slow waltz in the pink light of the sitting room.

Their dance is sedate and romantic and they dance easily and lightly together. As long as they dance, everything in Alice's world is safe.

Eve, who watches out for signs, thinks pink light is a sign that God is good.

Albert rises from the bed in his room where no-one can ask anything of him. The room looks on to the coal stack in the yard where dust settles everywhere – even on the white sheets Beauty hauls down from the line when they are dry and smell as fresh as new mown grass.

Albert turns off his radio because radios fill the air with music and chat and he doesn't want to hear the Dixie Cups singing 'Goin to the chapel and we're gonna get married; Goin to the chapel and we're gonna get married; Gee, I really love you and we're gonna get married; Goin' to the chapel of love.'

For years, Albert wanted to live in the city. He was confident he could have a different life and that he and his wife couldn't last. But Albert feels loose in Johannesburg - as if he were the only person there without a place. Although all he wants are ordinary days filled with ordinary work, Albert has begun to have a wild look about him.

It is two days before everything changes. Albert brings a tea tray and a pot of grape jam with a spoon sticking out of it into Eve's bedroom.

His face is reflected behind Eve's in the long mirror on the wardrobe door as if it were detached from his body and stuck on to the glass.

Eve asks, 'How is your boy, Albert? We won't give up on him, you know.'

Albert thinks, 'What would you like me to say?'

But he is polite so he says, 'Thank you. He is fine.'

'That's all right then.

And YOU, Albert, are YOU well?' Eve continues, anxious not to let the moment droop.

'Thank you. Why wouldn't I be?' Albert replies.

Albert is so thin he is hardly there but he has the face of man who knows all about the day, the night, the sky, water and air. Albert knows that we live as if we don't believe we are going to die.

Albert's son is called Jonah after the Bible story (which Albert says is not so much about God's salvation as about the power of an animal to provide shelter for a man – even an animal strange as this).

Jonah is the son who will know nothing about living with a family and will walk around with no memory of his father.

But, although life is harder for some, Albert's son will not be alone. When Albert's body goes to the darkness, his soul will decide not to join the spirits in the sky. It will settle, instead, in Jonah's heart, helping him prevent misfortune, protect against ill will and restore bad relations to good where he can.

When Jonah's face burns on a freezing night or when light on water startles him and makes him think about a swimming pool he has never seen, it will be his father's spirit within him, re-living his memories.

2

BEAUTY

CURRIED FISH

• • • • • • • • • • • • • • • • •

12 hake fillets; 3 large onions; 2 tablespoons curry powder; a few bay leaves and a few peppercorns; dessertspoon sugar; 1 and a half cups brown vinegar and 1 and a half cups water.

Dip fish first in flour then in egg and fry in hot oil – which is neither too deep nor too shallow. Drain. Leave. Slice onion then boil till soft. When onion is cold add vinegar, peppercorns, bay leaves, sugar, salt and curry powder and bring to the boil. Layer in a dish – first the fish then the onions. Cover and store in refrigerator for up to four days.

• • • • • • • • • • • • • • • • •

Saturday night. 9th December.

'Thank you. He is fine,' Beauty snorts, rolling Albert's words around her mind and smiling behind her eyes. 'You never really know Albert. You think you know him but he flies out of reach above the fruit trees.'

Most of the time, Beauty is quiet. Her lips move but no sound comes out – her voice more used to holding back than speaking. When she does speak, her voice is so soft it can't be captured on a page. Were Beauty's song to be played on a piano, it would be a piano with no strings.

Beauty likes cleaning because she doesn't have to talk to people and when she creeps past you, she hopes you don't care.

You never get close enough to Beauty to see if she is really pretty or how old she is – and she is inscrutable like an old walled city, but her skin is the colour of rain drenched earth and her eyes, the colour of mown grass.

Beauty has a poised, careful way of coming into a room and never troubles herself with anyone else's business.

'What I don't know won't hurt me,' she says.

Beauty is stuck in a time when nobody has any real power and is the first of her family to go into a white man's house. Looking at Beauty, you might be forgiven for wondering if the South African miracle could ever happen.

Albert says white men always obey authority and tells Beauty a joke.

'Beauty, how do you get white men out of a bar?

You call out "okie dokie white men – your time here is up".'

When the sun sets on the day, Beauty glides into her room (which alternately boils and freezes) in the yard where an old jacaranda offers shade. She shuts her door, crouches over her sewing machine (which she caresses like you caress a person you love) and watches the flow of stitches.

Beauty can stitch a path into oblivion. 'I love the way the stitches turn cloth into a shape,' she says.

Beauty's room seems frail and offers her little protection and the air inside it feels full of salt, somehow, like the sea she will never see.

She flicks a praying mantis off her cardigan, raises her hand to shield her eyes from the last of the day's brightness and stares into the garden.

There are rows of red hot pokers, cannas with glossy brown leaves and forbidden fruit sitting fat and ripe on trees: purple grapes, lime greengages, orange peaches, and lemons – all looking artificially coloured and meant for palates other than Beauty's.

'If I took fruit from the trees, what would I be stealing from – the earth?' she sighs.

Everyone else has friends, jokes and secrets. Beauty approaches trees to hold their trunks.

'Being alone requires such effort,' she tells Albert.

Beauty drinks tea with two sugars and counts days, thinking how they pass – sometimes quickly and sometimes slowly. Although her days are filled with scents like grape jam, simmering beets, apple jellies, pickled ox tongues and disinfectant, Beauty's happiness has nothing to do with perfume, the weather or flowers. Beauty simply tries to find ways of moving from dawn to dusk.

She scratches today off her calendar (it has taken such a long time for today to end) and takes her box of secrets from its hiding place.

(Beauty keeps her box of secrets locked. Although her name is written clearly on its lid, she often wonders if some elusive but important item has been taken from it. When Beauty thinks this way, her energy sags and her spirit hangs on her like an ill-fitting skirt).

Night falls quickly in Johannesburg. Beauty loves the silence the night brings and watches the dark come knocking on her windowpane, turning the garden black before she gets into her bed.

Beauty lies with her hands crossed over her chest, thinking of her father. (Beauty sleeps under a fan whose whirring blades fuse into a grey blur. Although she likes the breeze the fan creates, its noise disturbs her so she pulls her blanket up over her ears).

'I never knew my father,' she muses. 'I must have had one.'

Beauty does have a memory of her father but thinking of him makes her too sad to bear.

What Beauty has is an old memory which keeps coming to her – without forewarning – of an empty street save one woman looking out across the cars parked on either side of it as if they could bring someone back to her.

There are times when Beauty is in the middle of stacking saucepans or adjusting flowers in a vase (just so) and little butterflies come out all over her stomach. Beauty has tried praying but can't pray easily to someone she has never met.

'There is no need to bring all my experiences to God's attention, anyway,' she says, hoping – just to be safe – that God is a good listener.

'Apartheid is crumbling – don't you think?' venture some – their questioning heads tilted to the side. (And life being what it is, people soon move on to thinking of something else).

No-one guesses that Beauty's greatest fear is of people taking from her the ordinary things which make her human.

No-one guesses that Beauty's greatest fear is of people seeing her simply as black.

On Albert's days off, Beauty creeps into his room to smell the Moonshine, picture Albert's fluttering hands and bearded face staring out at her from the wall.

She wraps Albert's blanket around her before folding it away and cleans the room (where dust has settled) till sweat runs down her face and she can hear Albert's returning footsteps sounding through the yard.

Beauty longs to meet someone she can love and a part of her is always waiting – waiting for a face at her window, a figure in the distance, for days to end, for washing to dry and for Albert to return home.

'The worst is waiting for things to change when you know that nothing ever changes,' says Beauty, 'or to be waiting for someone who never appears.'

Beauty was a young girl when she left her family and will feel young until Eve dies. Then, she will return to the place of her birth as an old woman with a hunched back and a need to explain to the villagers that 'whites are also people.'

Albert says, 'If a venomous black mamba drinks water, the water turns to poison inside him. If a kudu buck drinks water, the water becomes horns.

A venomous snake can't make horns.

This is destiny.'

Beauty's life is caught up in Eve's.

'I was put on this earth to meet Eve,' says Beauty.

Eve is Beauty's destiny.

(When they leave the white house, Beauty and Eve – who, by then, will have the comfortable air of friends between whom a lifetime has passed, will wait with their suitcases for a taxi to take them to their new home. The strange middle-aged woman who seems to spend her life hanging over the garden wall as if she were growing up it, will talk at length about something like stars or spas and enquire after Eve's health.

Eve will think, 'Why are you staring? Where are your manners?'

She will say, 'It doesn't matter. At least, it doesn't matter to you.'

Eve will leave the white house with a puzzled face and her hand in Beauty's which she will mistake for Alice's.

After Eve dies, her bed will be left unmade, the dishes unwashed and the plants neglected – just so.

Beauty will plant a 'yesterday, today and tomorrow' to mark Eve's passing. She will explain that she, alone, knows that the purple flowers – the yesterdays – are Eve's favourites).

The lights are out in the white house but a fafi game is going on in the yard. Alice has drifted into the state of near sleep where you believe you are still awake.

She thinks of unexpected flowers growing through pavement cracks and of crickets flying over the trees they seem to shape with their wings and she feels a surge of the same freedom as if, at any time, she herself might fly into the sky.

Taking with her this feeling of lightness, Alice boards a train bound for Durban, last outpost of the British Empire, and travels the distance past goldmines and the rocky ridges of the Witwatersrand for her first glimpse of the sea and the smell of salt in the wind.

What actually happens is that Alice lies in the dark, still as a swimming pool, thinking of the night's shadows, its random shapes and the buds which turn to flowers in the moonlight catching you unawares.

How could Alice not be happy?

She has whole families of lizards, dragonflies and silkworms around her. Alice, alone, knows that a bee's nest is lodged in the nectarine tree.

It will take a while for Alice to understand the tendency in her family to lie about each other like keeping from Eve the news of Oscar's death because there is only so much a person can take.

Beauty is angry.

She lies in bed worrying about the little white child with the earth coloured eyes spending so much time on the side lines of life. There are times when Beauty would like to ask Alice what she is thinking but she wonders if Alice sees her as someone who is always cleaning houses and she can't find the words.

'Ay, ay, ay,' thinks Beauty. 'This place is full of trouble. Trouble waits in the blue veins (the light seems to shine through) on Eve's hands, it sleeps under Oscar's helmet and it reclines in the dust on Albert's bedroom floor.'

(Albert – who has no idea what Beauty is like 'as a person'- says that an angry little white boy once threw his toys on to a fire. A sprinkling of ash rose from the flames to the sky and formed the Milky Way. Albert says, 'beware of anger. Its marks may be indelible.')

The Milky Way winks Beauty to sleep, lighting the prayers passing from her head to Alice's heart.

Sunday 10th December. Not much going on.

The night was long but nothing changed.

Life is slow in the 1960s. Time is marked out in swimming pool laps and some people just sit silent, watching days go by. In the houses of privilege, little action other than cleaning takes place and there are days when vacuum cleaners are the only moving things.

Mornings billow into afternoons and afternoons into nights. The postman delivers the mail every day, gardeners catch stray leaves in nets every day, blue-rinsed ladies dawdle in shopping malls, bridge parties roll out to fill spaces and groceries are bought, packed away and bought again.

But the sixties in Johannesburg are not as people picture them in England.

There are flowers everywhere, people wear flares, 'wet-look' and acid colours and make their own necklaces out of Zulu beads. They listen to the Beatles and Simon and Garfunkel, read Alan Ginsberg and Jack Kerouac, watch 'Easy Rider' and go on protest marches – but there doesn't seem to be much freedom around.

Over tea and toast, when the sky is green, there is not a star to be seen and the clouds move around without purpose, Eve is waiting for something to happen. She is bored with acquiring and arranging and the day feels tired.

Eve opens the dining room window and is listening to the sprinklers, distant shrieks, police sirens and laughter when two bedraggled birds flop from their nest in the tree outside on to the floor by her feet.

'A gift – a sign,' thinks Eve, 'but of what? That God is good?'

Eve continues, 'What have I done? I must stop seeing signs in everything'- before realising she is only an observer.

(Once in every lifetime everything seems to have something to say to you; a row of red hot pokers straight as you like, the shapes the clouds make, the patterns of leaves lying on pavements or winds blowing so strong, birds can't fly in them.

Eve longs for a sign – a rainbow or a butterfly on a buddleia – to signify that God is listening and she feels unhappy when her fear that life is nothing more than a series of improbable accidents is confirmed).

Beauty, who carries being invisible to an extreme, stands in the doorway, watching. She knows the lives of housewives and their houses. She knows Eve.

Eve feels safe with Beauty. She knows she can say anything, that it will be stored away in Beauty's mind and that she will not be judged.

Eve takes it for granted that Beauty will be there, and asks (when talking to Beauty feels the same as talking to herself),

'Did I tell you, Beauty dear, that I was once the second best player in the netball team?'

Eve remembers what shooting goal feels like even if she can no longer manage it. She still has some of her past dexterity and grace and knows that disappointment is easy enough to bury down if you have to. If she speaks of good fortune, she follows it with a three times spit and says, 'pah, pah, pah' – because you know how easily good can turn bad.

Eve allows herself a cigarette a day. When she drags on her cigarette, she gives these thoughts her puzzled attention while peering into the rising twists of smoke. She then flicks ash into the stomach of the ballerina-shaped ashtray Oscar won at a fair.

('Why NOT smoke?' she answers an imaginary interrogator – when asked about her habit).

Of everything Eve has fought for, she has fought hardest for acclaim; for people to acknowledge her gift to the world as more than a colour co-ordinated shimmer – for people to say, 'Ah. There goes Eve: competent Eve.'

'Yes, Beauty,' Eve continues, narrowing her eyes and talking quickly in case what she thinks Beauty is about to say is not what she wants to hear, 'I was as close to representing our good province as I am to you now.'

Eve pokes the air with her hands to give a sense of the distance and reflects on the fact that her netball playing was abandoned – along with so many other half-realised ambitions – just at the point of her being chosen for the team.

'I have no regrets, but my life could have been as perfect as the silver teaspoon you see on this tray,' she says (her voice dying down to a whisper so that almost nothing can be heard), 'and I know what I am talking about.'

Beauty's fixed smile suggests she is not entirely present. She wonders how anyone can be so beautiful and so troubled at the same time.

'Life can be messy, Beauty, but the course of it can be changed by nothing more than the decision to walk across a room.'

When the sun is too hot, Eve lies in the green chill of the grass or dives into the brightly tiled swimming pool. Eve is still agile and will look like a netball player till the day she dies but she does not tell anyone how much time she has on her hands.

Beauty checks the coils of sticky yellow fly paper hanging in the kitchen then goes outside, picks a leaf off a fig tree and uses it to wipe bird dropping off the veranda.

Something surprises Beauty every time she gets out the vacuum cleaner. You would think that nothing mattered more to her than the families of ladybirds which come from nowhere and settle on lampshades but, the truth is that Beauty drags her cleaning around like the excess pounds behind which she hides.

On the shelves lining Oscar's study, you read the story of his life. There are books such as Maimonides's 'Guide For the Perplexed' and Martin Buber's 'I and Thou' from Oscar's religious study, Grey's 'Anatomy' and Freud's 'Studies of Hysteria' from his time as a medical student, 'The Sex Life of Savages' and 'The Well of Loneliness' from around the same time, then Winston Churchill's 'The Second World War' which speaks for itself, Olive Schreiner's 'The Story of an African Farm' and Sir Percy Fitzpatrick's 'Jock of the Bushveld' which gave Oscar a window on African life and stories such as Rudyard Kipling's 'Kim' and 'Dombey and Son' by Dickens.

The books' grave expression disturbs Beauty.

In the special stillness of the morning, Beauty picks one up thinking she will read just a few lines, but puts it back in its place and runs her feathers up and down its spine instead.

Beauty dabs the mirrors in the house with a wet cloth (being careful not to look too long at her reflection in the glass); first, the silver mirror in the bedroom which seems to blush as the sun shifts over it, then the hall mirror framed by carved wooden feathers, then the oval mirror above the piano reflecting the brass camel with the lucky hump.

Up and down she cleans while the clock in the kitchen tells her how slowly time is passing. Then she checks herself to see what she is wearing, joins six of her fellow cooks and cleaners in the back seat of a taxi meant for two and is driven away from the houses in rows with street lights and running water to the stony tracks of the township where just rows are a luxury and where strange stories and wounded hearts reside.

Johannesburg is decades away from its peaceful revolution which is decades away from the city's slide down from the top of Africa's financial elite and decades away from Nelson Mandela's death.

'Never mind,' say some (who have read about poor people in books) 'that a mere twenty miles away from our suburbs, you can touch the (corrugated iron) roof of your neighbour's house. Never mind that the goldmines have stripped the soil of water. Never mind that the drains have not been completed. Never mind that the levels of water in the pumps are so low people have only drops to drink. And never mind that the water is so polluted it is better not to drink it, anyway.'

Beauty has no sense of direction, does not know where she is going and worries about something dreadful happening.

'I had better prepare myself,' she thinks. 'You never know what will come next.'

The taxi is full of secrets. Through the cigar-shaped back window Beauty sees the department store (where the lift attendants wear white gloves) pass by, then the botanical gardens (where brides who pose for photographs seem to grow out of the ground), then the park on the edge of the city where white children are afraid to play.

(Her mother warned her about strange people in public parks so Alice is afraid of parks and wonders who these people are. But Oscar says, 'Parks have nothings to do with 'people', Alice. Parks are about grass, trees and a few bushes.')

Because the taxi is speeding – and speeding into the dark – a creeping, gripping, fluttering something settles in Beauty's stomach and won't go away. She has to lace her fingers together to stop them shaking and sits with her legs intertwined with those of her fellow passengers – whose hair is hidden under the starched servants' scarves they pull off when they enter the township. Beauty can smell diesel and Koo apricot jam.

Beauty tries conversation.

'My jobs are done – except not. I wake in the middle of the night thinking of the work I have to do because there is a limit to the amount of mess around the house I can put up with.' (There is no mess in the house at all).

Beauty's voice is surprisingly deep and low so people have to strain to hear her.

'Look at the sky,' she continues. 'It looks white and strange with blue clouds strung across it like washing... The guard geese in the yard are cranky (geese with sunshine on their wings and clacking beaks patrol the white house) I see faces in the flowerbeds...'

Beauty's feelings can't be put into words – and might never be – and her thoughts are scattered like pins all over the floor. But Beauty is not as different from others as you might think; she feels what other people feel even if she would never say what they say.

Beauty does not want white people's lives and is quite glad not to have their opinions; she does not even understand white people well enough to gauge their ages.

What Beauty does know is that as the years pass, her eyes seem to be growing greener like the algae on a fish pond – and less able to see.

The landscape is making Beauty melancholy (certain shades of red brick caught in sunlight bring back sad memories for her) not because of the late afternoon sun on the walls she passes but because of the lives of the people behind them. She looks towards the driver:

'Tomorrow night, the first thing I'll do is cook Durban curry with sultanas, bananas, tomatoes and peppers.'(Eve says rickshaw boys in beaded head-dresses line the Durban promenade and sharks swim in the ocean behind them).

It is hard to tell if the driver has been listening to anything – or if he cares. He looks wasted because he has been driving into the sunset and has had to tilt his head all the way so he can get his eyes into shadow.

They arrive at the township. Beauty checks her looks in the car window.

Messages from the Church of Zion welcome them. The driver breaks under a message suggesting that 'If you have Faith you can do anything' – and narrowly misses a Putco bus packed with gardeners.

The taxi's headlamps pick out nothing – then, tethered goats, red foot falcons, the peeling bark of eucalyptus trees and people selling hubcaps, dagga and skin-whitening creams come into view as the seven women lurch toward the windscreen.

Dust balls – which Beauty is glad to say are not her concern – blow down the streets, getting into Beauty's nose and mouth. She stares at people who mean nothing to her and hides away the thought that she would love to follow whatever it is they are saying.

'I don't come here looking for work or trouble', she says to an imaginary interrogator of her own, 'I have a sewing machine and paraffin lamp to collect and more secret gifts to deliver.'

(Does the township change Beauty? Yes, for a while and then, not.

When she hurries back to the place where the lawns and the empty stillness begin, she expects the white house to have changed in the same way. She is always pleased to find it has not).

At the end of the day Beauty returns to her room in the yard with a headache and wonders if it is because she stepped under a ladder on her way into the sewing machine shop.

Sunday, December 10th: late afternoon.

Oscar and Jack come into view turning from black spots into men wearing hats.

Jack is a dark, slow person who shares responsibility for the care of the flowers. Circumstances have dulled Jack and he spends most of his time sitting on the grass with his trilby on his head wondering when fruit will ripen. He lumbers beside Oscar, breathing heavily and watching Oscar's face so silently and so close, he thinks it is part of his own.

Black men and white men have centuries ahead of them – Oscar just thinks about feeling older now his helmet is too large for his head.

The sun lowers itself on to the men's faces and unsettles them.

Heat like this drives men's dreams from their heads and wipes the edges off things. Birds land wherever they go with such quiet exhaustion, you would think all flying had taken the day off.

The garden is usually as rousing as a hymn. Albert sees it as a place to dream and wander, Alice, a place for insects and slugs and Oscar a place to gather up the past.

But if the garden were a song today, it would be played on a cello making muffled sounds beneath the trees.

Oscar is not in the mood for Sunday's bright sunshine. He does not want to complicate something as beautiful as life but can't help reflecting how he might have been different or things gone differently. Oscar wants nothing more or less than for time to move slowly. He does not want the past back.

He closes his eyes and thinks of all that sits between him and his former life and thinks, 'my early life was not better than this one.'

Oscar has faced so many challenges and changes, he wonders if he was a particular victim of history or if he mismanaged situations – or if all this really matters. He pushes these thoughts – with his helmet – to the back of his head.

Oscar thinks of life and its meaning and of death and its meaning and sighs, 'One can never know the truth about people who have no voice.'

Oscar still speaks in a formal way – his speech suffused with religious study.

'Am I becoming South African?' he wonders, 'Does the accent of my birth still cling to my tongue? Even if I alter my accent, I cannot evade my beginnings.'

Oscar notices the many things about life – about people, animals and the weather – which make living difficult for some. He sits in his garden with his grandfather's hand on his shoulder and wonders if he is missing out.

Oscar can't help himself. He is who he is.

(Albert tells the story of the antelope who stepped out of his skin one morning and into that of a monkey. The monkey's skin felt tight on the antelope and the antelope itched all day. When the antelope reclaimed his own skin, the sun had burned it to biltong leaving him neither antelope nor monkey.

'You are who you are,' says Albert. 'You are not on this earth to borrow another life.')

Oscar is sixty and tinnitus aside, is fit, lean and still with hope. When he looks at all the tomorrows stretching ahead of him, he wonders if they will be different from his yesterdays.

'Beginnings happen throughout a life but there are times when you think you are starting afresh only to find yourself going backwards all over again,' he sighs.

(The strange middle-aged woman who lurks at the bottom of the garden and leans against the wall like wilting bougainvillea is watching out for things which might go wrong. Her watchfulness is as familiar and as painful to her as the prick of a cactus spine.

She says things like 'time flies', 'carpe diem' and 'life is a mystery' and because she sees things no-one else sees, she looks in corners for black people and Communists. Most of the time, Oscar raises his hand pleasantly when she passes.

Oscar is thinking of his rescue from Dunkirk when she asks him a question which sounds like 'Are there differences between... never to be mended?' but the afternoon breeze blows some of her words away.

Oscar, who knows she makes everything up, cups his hand around his good ear and thinks, 'there are people I pity just for being who they are.'

He coughs and waits until he stops before saying, 'We don't see things as they are.')

Oscar twice suggests to Jack, 'Sit on the grass beside me. Jack? Sit beside me. Jack, let us rest for a while.'

Difficulties have altered both men – and not entirely for the better – but the garden does all it can to repair broken people. It asks nothing about a man's religion or the colour of his skin. Jack, for one, manages to be happy just by being in the garden and not speaking much.

Jack does not look people in the eye. When he talks to you he often looks at the sky and your eyes are always seeking out his eyes.

Gardening can leave you feeling stiff. Jack walks beside Oscar, swaying from side to side and Oscar feels the stiffness of Jack's movements in his own joints.

Most of the time Jack moves only because it is necessary to move but there are times when Jack walks for hours after sunset when there is a wind cooling the streets.

There are times when Jack walks along streets so deserted, they are little affected by the changing seasons.

There are times when the nights are so hot Jack drags his matrass into the yard. There are times when a night in Jack's life can mean going to sleep (like a night watchman – with only a blanket for cover) for less than an hour. And there are times when Jack goes to sleep when he hears the birds waking.

'My journey from bed to garden takes only a minute,' he explains, removing his battered trilby and placing it down beside Oscar's helmet.

Johannesburg weather is moderate – hot and cold, just so – but this is not a summer about green grass, blue sky, singing cicadas and coloured drinking straws peeping out of glasses. This summer, houses melt, paintings fade and agapanthus go limp. The heat pushes you backwards, brings with it a thousand discomforts, inconveniences, broken hearts and shames because no-one has energy to do anything about anything. Newspapers write about the heat wave – the worst since 1948 – and people will say 'remember the heat wave?' for years to come.

Sunday 10th December is one of the hottest days of the year.

Oscar scans his life; all is as it should be. Eve's mirror reflects her rainbows, Jack is beside him and the scent of roses fills the air. Last night Albert stood in a shaft of moonlight, talking about God's painters in heaven who mix the yellow of the sand and the white of the sea's foam to make stars.

But there are times when the burden of history and propriety lie heavy on Oscar – when nothing is comfortable and it is too much for him to bear all that suffering and deprivation, all those battles and the endless moving on to escape danger.

A strange shift is taking place.

Everything seemed possible. Everything seemed fine.

Now Oscar sees with doctor's eyes that this cannot last and tears cloud his vision. (The tears are so unexpected, he wonders if they are his).

'I must be tired,' he says to Jack, 'that is why I am crying. I shall sleep well tonight.'

'We may as well all cry,' thinks Jack – although he doesn't know for what.

Jack's skin is the blackest but it glows with light and he has the name 'William' tattooed on his left shoulder. Because everyone in the house carries with them the aura of another half known-about life, no-one asks why.

Jack does not usually think about what is happening around him but he does think all white people understand each other because they look alike and speak the same language.

Till he came to work in the white house, he had not seen such beautiful flowers and he acts like a moving part of the garden, saying, 'my life began and will end among the flowers.'

If Jack were Oscar he might think, 'If it all stopped tomorrow, what would I have to show for it?'

But he is not. His thoughts don't go this way.

(Because Oscar is the closest person in the world to Jack, Jack often imagines himself speaking like Oscar – using words like 'satisfactory' and 'fertile'. But Jack does not embark on debates).

What Jack does is tell the truth – he can't himself.

Jack feels compelled to reveal everything – even if it means having to say things like 'there is porridge on your chin' or to ask 'why are you limping?'

But you can't tell the truth all the time.

Jack tells the time (as much as you can) by looking at the shadows the trees cast out on to the grass.

When Oscar leaves for the hospital on weekday mornings or when he returns to the white house, proud Jack knows, from his shadows, that it is that time.

When Albert's face is reflected in the mirror, three times behind Eve's, Jack nods because it is THAT time – black shapes, like cartoons on the lawn, have told him so.

And when Oscar's or Albert's movements don't conform to the garden's shadows, Jack has to sit very still and wonder where his friends have gone wrong or climb to the top of the compost heap to think.

Oscar and Jack rarely laugh together but when they do – at the weather or a worm or a weed– Jack likes it because it makes him feel as if Oscar is his friend.

A frog jumps on to Jack's foot, tickles him and makes him smile. Jack reaches out an uncertain hand and places it on Oscar's – just for a second – and this gesture is as close as Jack will ever come to an expression of intimacy.

Doctor and gardener want little of each other. They are happy to know each other in outline rather than detail. They crouch together talking about how different this year is from the last and the flowers most likely to bloom soon and the patterns of the shrubs till the night comes at them from the distance.

Jack sometimes dreams he is helping Oscar climb down from the top of a tree but failing for not being strong enough for the task. All that remain of Oscar are his glasses which float toward the sun.

Jack also dreams of being in the right street but the wrong garden and, although there are flowers blooming under his fingers, he is caught in grass growing waist high and can't mow it. He looks around and asks 'where am I?' but can't find himself in the long stretches of green.

What a relief, then, to walk outside and see the daffodils peeping out of the stripes in the just mown lawn of the white house.

There are twenty years to go till a new century opens its eyes. Oscar will not see it.

When Oscar dies, he will be buried in the Jewish cemetery which resembles a leafy garden with rose beds at the sides. Fate will intervene, as usual, and bring sunshine to the cemetery just like it brought sunshine to Oscar on his first day in this city when the glittering ranks of roofs looked like marching soldiers and reminded him of the war.

Oscar will be buried beside Eve and husband and wife will dance rumba, samba and fox-trot in the land of the dead and for the rest of time.

Jack does not want to worry about dying.

'I know about the dead people,' he tells Albert.

But he thinks, 'I do not wish to be one of them.'

All Jack wants is to go to a place where people will wait on him.

5

ALBERT

BEST PEACH MOONSHINE

• • • • • • • • • • • • • • • •

*Mash ripe yellow peaches in a barrel. Leave for two weekends to rot
and ferment. Allow gases to escape but please keep insects out. Heat
the peaches to just before boiling and when the peach mash stops
bubbling, strain and serve.*

• • • • • • • • • • • • • • • •

Monday, 11th December Albert's birthday.

This is the time when Albert spends Monday nights gambling in the
township.

Something shifts in the land of the dead people. A soul which
has travelled the distance from Lithuania to the Africa alters position. It could be that, in the past, this once good soul left its body
and because no vigil was kept over it or prayers said, it came to
cause trouble in the world.

In the dark black of apartheid (when – difficult though it is to believe – the government bans jazz for being subversive), all South
Africans who breathe music, have to find ways of making sounds
which have never been heard before. Unfamiliar and hypnotic

drumbeats, eerie solos on Jew's harps and a cappella choruses rise up from the township, stirring the spirits living in the sky.

Beauty is sewing in her room when Albert plays a song on his pennywhistle – a siren song which lures her out.

'Some mornings, Beauty, you look like you have come up through deep water,' Albert says.

Although Beauty wonders if Albert is real (and if anyone knows him), they have developed – without speaking – a certain order and harmony of washing and drying, stacking and packing away.

Beauty tries to get Albert to say something to which she can reply.

'So, I see the grapes are ripe now?'

Albert carries on playing pennywhistle.

'You don't believe me?' she continues.

Then, she suggests, 'Turn around, Albert. Is that Alice sitting among the flowers on the top branch of the purple tree?

Do you believe in such things as souls, Albert?'

'Yes,' says Albert.

'What's wrong with you, Albert?'

Beauty fears for Albert's position in the world and her face falls.

(But if anyone were to ask, 'What is it, Beauty?' She would reply, 'Nothing.')

Albert and Beauty look at each other.

She thinks, 'He is different. He is not from around here.'

Albert says, 'I am not from around here. Did I tell you of the black man who wanted to be white?'

Albert speaks as if addressing the sun above. He often suspects God has a special purpose for him, but he wonders what it is.

'He bathed in the milk of stars,' he continues, 'but his black soul pined for his music – the music of his ancestors – and left his body for another. The black man became white but lost his music.'

Does Albert's soul pine for his music?

At least Albert sees and hears the world.

Before anyone else, Albert feels the first flutter of spring and summer following behind it. When winters are cool and listless, he is the first to feel the shoots below ground clamouring for more than the sun's meagre show.

Albert sees Eve's blue veined fingers turn the radio dial around and around on bored afternoons and the deepening furrows on Oscar's brow. And Albert, alone, knows that a particular show of pink light could be fairies, hatched from eggs left in the grass, flying by to do their work in the world.

But Albert is lonely and has learned to keep his loneliness, his fear and his longing for the stillness of his room.

When the floors are clean, the windows washed and the woman in the green dress departed, Albert makes Moonshine for his dreams and his wife.

Everyone knows about apartheid but what people don't know is that Albert spends most of his time fearing rejection.

What would Albert say – if asked?

'My loneliness is as close to me as my shadow. Because I am afraid I am not up to much, I have never really been good at making friends. I have always believed in love but if I love somebody, they should not feel obliged to think the same way.'

Not a day passes when Albert does not think of his wife. He allows himself to walk with her in the sand and take her hand. He does not need to say 'I always meant to come back to you' because he knows she knows. Albert's wife is the reason for his stories and his pennywhistle cries out about her unquestioning manner and delicate skin which made his every touch feel like he was causing harm.

Albert's wife, who cannot accept that Albert has no further use for her, tries to move from season to season – from birth to death – without unnecessary sentiment. She does not ask questions. She knows Albert is not like other men. She says Albert's leaving marked the end of her youth and she always wonders what he would think or say about her now.

When she thinks of her husband she sees him forever young. She pictures a thin man who cannot stand still and she prefers to think this way than to worry about an older man who might be in the grip of an ancestral spirit or trying to keep sane. Albert's wife has purple eyes like katorba grapes, a giving spirit, a soft step and has resigned herself to her life.

(She lives with her brother who is a lazy man with a troubled head and no teeth. He does not have plans for the day, for the week, for his life and because nothing spreads before him, he is determined to do something to stop the unfulfilled longing which gnaws at his soul.

What can he do? What does he want? What does he have in mind?

If he could answer these questions, he would not be where he is. Little does he know that he will one day go mad after endless nights of insomnia in which he is hounded by the sounds of wailing sirens).

It is a long time since Albert and his wife were together.

If Albert saw her now he would find her as dark and shadowy as he remembered and with an almost soundless physical presence.

If Albert saw her now, he might say, 'I always thought I would come back to you – even in hindsight, even if only in the still of my mind. I could come back to you, you know, for you are the first love of my heart.'

Albert thanks his ancestors' spirits in his yellow room before going to sleep. Albert has no wish to be known for insolence to the spirits, so he obeys their calling. He does not seek greatness: Albert acknowledges whatever gift life gives him when he has it in his hand. And Albert's face is sometimes shadowy as if the feet of his ancestors had made their way across it.

Albert will tell stories and play Kwela music against every influence and until his world breaks down.

Although Albert does not always remember and although he has given up trying to understand, Albert hopes he has not given up.

During the war, and at the time Oscar was marching along Dunkirk's sands waiting for rescue, a young orphan from Guilin embarked on a journey too long and painful to describe. He ended up in Johannesburg, trading the green wet of paddy fields for the yellow dust of goldmines. (The new landscape was so familiar he thought he might have known it long ago).

The young man was lucky enough to buy a small house in the township, a large maroon coloured car and a life lived as far away from Chairman Mao as possible.

Twenty-five years on, his son, known in the suburbs as 'the Chinaman', king of gamblers, man of careful manners, sweeps down the road leading from the township to the white house, parks his maroon Ford Cortina (with seat covers made of wooden beads) a few doors down from it and waits to give value to Albert's dreams. (He never parks his car directly outside the house and you know he has arrived only by the sound of the running engine).

Albert plays fafi with men half his age and twice as strong and fears what will happen if he stops. The men smoke, drink Moonshine and swap stories about work, women and white men.

For the time being, Albert is lucky. He keeps a winning streak.

He weaves tales of love and sends people and animals pouring out of his head in such exotic formations and equations that the Chinaman is full of enterprise and delight. (The Chinaman has a long talon on the middle finger of his left hand, scratches his chest with it when nervous and – even when asking others 'what's wrong?' – has fractions frolicking in his brain).

Albert dreamed of a white faced king (value 1) riding his bicycle to the moon (value 9). Then Albert dreamed that the Chinaman chased him across the swimming pool. He looked up and saw Jack's trilby moving slowly above the privet hedge.

'Help me Jack,' Albert cried.

But Jack nodded a greeting to the earth, looked away and back to Albert before disappearing into a daffodil leaving Albert – now a fish (13) – swimming in a pool until he reached the sea.

Because there is never enough money for a taxi (and there are few white people who understand the fear of not finding any money at all at the bottom of your purse), Albert pays for a ride in the Chinaman's car with Moonshine and the story of a dream. He slides into the back seat and the Chinaman – like a chauffeur – sits up front.

'In a perfect world, I would be anywhere but here,' thinks the Chinaman.

'Because I can't keep money, it doesn't mean I don't think about it,' thinks Albert.

The Chinaman is used to the pain in peoples' eyes. He scratches his chest and adds 26 (water) to 7 (robbers).

Albert plans to win some money in a place where the old, the injured and the jobless (who make music on mbiras) move forward by squeezing sideways through tiny spaces – or until the police carry them away.

Because he knows that the Chinaman brings with him the taste of a wider, unfamiliar world which can swallow you up at any time (and that once you've turned towards the township, you've committed to another life), Albert feels unsettled.

With his heart beating like the thumping of gumboots when the miners dance, (stamping down on the sand and rattling dustbin lids), Albert prepares himself and the journey begins. Albert is afraid of how weak he feels – of how little life he feels within.

Various images drift through Albert's brain. He passes the time talking to the Chinaman about this and that. He talks about silent Beauty, Alice on her mushroom, Ruth's face in her mirror and steady, sturdy, time telling Jack.

What does the driver think of the heat wave, the raindrops hot as bathwater and the melted tarmac sticking to his tyres? Any subject will do. (But there are some Albert holds back).

Albert talks about his first years in the city where he arrived from a farm with a blanket in his hand and poetry in his head. He talks about things he wanted to do but which now seem improbable.

He says he is well on the way to living the life of luxury he had planned for himself back then and has no strength left for cleaning. Albert says he has no strength.

The driver keeps to a steady forty miles an hour but, because the traffic is bad for a Monday, Albert wonders if he should have taken another route.

He says, 'I am here to tell you I feel as if I don't know anything. I wonder if I have lost my place in the world.'

'What do you want me to do?' asks the Chinaman.

A feeble thought tries to find space in Albert's mind.

'What would my father say if he could see me now?'

But the thought dries up like a stream in a summer drought.

'Wherever I am, I cannot escape myself. I may do wrong but can't find a way out so I have to go on acting as if I were right. Although I don't tell anyone my whole story, any doubts about me are held only by those who have never met me,' Albert says, coming as close to a confession of something as he will ever come.

'May I ask you a personal question – as we have got this far? Why is it all sad in your car tonight?'

But the driver is silent because peoples' secrets aren't defined or their feelings easy to recognize. He fears a danger has entered the evening. He catches his own furtive eyes in the rear-view mirror and busies himself adding 9 (the moon) to 15 (prostitutes) to 21 (elephants) to 22 (ships) to 3 (sailors) to 28 (small fish) to 26 (bees) to 30 (a priest).

He thinks of the day he can give it all up and return to China with cash in his pockets and pride on his face before a new danger – the threat of change – engulfs him.

The sky which shelters Albert, shelters his wife. She has lost Albert but something far away makes her shiver – although the night is hot. She feels restless and as if a force is pulling her upward from her state of half-life. She remembers young Albert and, with extraordinary clarity, pictures the older man leaving the white house, patting his pockets and sliding into a car.

Albert arrives in the township. (No-one has a real identity here because all are living the same life and it is hard to be sure when you have arrived at any particular home). The wind blows bits of plastic bag and cardboard box about.

'I want to walk. The evening is so lovely,' he says and jumps out of the car. He shakes the driver's hand and thanks him. (He would like to find respect in the driver's eyes – to have the car door opened for him. He would like to reply, 'Thank you – you are kind.')

The Chinaman wishes him the best game of his life and says 'be strong.' He has to hurry because Albert's need for conversation has made him late.

Although the Chinaman doesn't mean what he says – these are just words – they sound like a warning.

Albert walks down streets with their smells of summer and sounds of Kwela music until he reaches the house where his family live and rests his head against the outside wall.

'There is always an evening when you realize the summer is too hot and the traffic too fast,' he thinks.

Albert makes coffee and eats bread and jam. He tastes his wife's sweetness in the jam and sees her dark eyes in the coffee.

Albert's family worry only about surviving – having something to eat and an unbroken roof – and pay little attention to each other. They are too busy to remark on the beauty of the evening or the majesty of flower heads full of water after the rain and they have nothing like a clear intimation of what is about to happen right there on their floor.

Albert sees a sliver of polished lino (between an overturned box and a fridge so small you could carry it under your arm) and asks,

'May I lie down on the floor for the night – or under a tree – if you have the shade of a tree to spare?'

Albert plans to play fafi, thank his family then go to sleep but he sees they are afraid – although they cannot tell him why.

Albert looks through his glasses (which have slipped to the end of his nose) down the road leading to a field filled with broken beer bottles and the skeletons of cars and is startled by a shadow cutting out his light: a terrible surprise.

Albert's hand is half-way to his face – and before he can take off his glasses, his wife's brother (who has not spoken to anyone for several years) thrusts a knife into his back with appalling slowness, ignoring Albert's pleas to return to the white house or, at least, to live just a moment longer.

Not a thing to be done.

Recognition dawns on Albert – then incredulity then horror.

Pain fires up his whole body, stunning him into silence.

Now Albert is alive, now he is not: the walk across the room which changes everything.

Albert slumps down as quietly as heat rising from a swimming pool and his ordinary life flies out of the window just as his coffee spills all over the floor.

Albert dies on a Monday night, a nondescript night of no grandeur or significance – like a Saturday, for instance.

Albert dies on the night of his forty-third birthday and all night long the crickets chirp on the trees which stand against the sky like cardboard cut-outs as if nothing has happened in the world.

'Why did you hate Albert?' People ask the murderer.

'No reason.'

'What were you thinking? Did Albert's happiness result in your unhappiness?'

'God knows.'

'What is the problem? What were you afraid of? What sort of a thing is this?'

'It is the only thing.'

'Why?'

'No time, no room, no food, no light, no chair...'

At midnight, Albert's brother-in-law (whose toothless gums deepen his look of secrecy) leaves the township in time to catch the last bus – which has three other sleeping people on it who do not know him. He is wrapped in a blanket and wipes his blade.

He acted in a way no-one can understand – except to say that he could not help it.

4
NOISE

PERI-PERI RUB

• • • • • • • • • • • • • • • •

3 red peppers, quarter of a cup of lemon juice, lime juice, quarter of a cup of sunflower oil, tablespoon cayenne pepper, tablespoon paprika, teaspoon salt and teaspoon crushed garlic.

Mix all ingredients to a smooth paste. Rub the mixture on to fish or meat and marinate in a bowl for at least 30 minutes before cooking.

• • • • • • • • • • • • • • • •

Monday, 11th December.

That was Saturday and Saturday night, Sunday and Sunday night, Monday morning and Monday night. No-one can go back to the people they were on Friday.

Life – and the business of making do, loving, suffering, gossiping and not understanding – flows on. If this year is different from other years, it is different by only a little.

People have shops to go to, plants to plant, sick to heal and dice to throw. People will sit in traffic, come home, go to bed and start all over again the next day.

Albert will know none of this.

For Albert, all has gone quiet.

Little thinking that Albert will not bring up her cup of tea with milk at sunrise because a knife is lodged in his back Eve draws the curtains on a ghostly garden. The sky is starless – and neutral – as if all light which bore witness to the crime, retreated.

In the stillness of their room, Eve is wondering whether anyone would notice if she went mad. Her fingers travel along the dark sheets till they find her husband's and their hands interlock.

Down in the kitchen, Beauty stacks away the saucepans, pulls shut the fly-screen door leading to the yard, walks in to her room, opens her box of secrets and her sewing machine.

On the outskirts of the city a train's lonely whistle echoes through the sky.

Silence descends on the township. To report the crime is a waste of time.

The people surrounding Albert say nothing for some seconds before screaming out something like, 'Death has returned once again to take its chances.'

The Chinaman (late, now, for his appointment) walks up to them – straight past men planning other crimes. At a loss, for a moment, as to what to do next, he tries to think what they are staring at and why for so long.

'If someone is dying, why do you want to watch him die? And is this dying person completely dead yet?' he asks.

Because he puts fantastical interpretations on things, he acts on the suspicion that death must have knocked on a different door and wakes the neighbours.

The light increases by the minute and with it comes the news which spreads through the township – passing from those who saw Albert to those who missed him.

Currents of gossip pull along even those struggling not to be involved.

'Did the township kill him?'

'Did everybody kill him?'

'Who knows if there was a motive?'

'Why shouldn't he die? His life was such a struggle.'

'Something similar happened to someone the night before.'

'Where were you at the time?'

'I shouldn't speak ill of the dead, but…'

'New tragedies happen daily – couldn't we just go on as if nothing had happened?'

'Has this genuinely happened?'

'This could have happened to us.'

'You couldn't make this up.'

Some people say Albert was a gentle victim. Some say he dabbled in places and situations he did not understand. Some say Albert's inability to hold on to money meant Moonshine was a minor vice. Some say Albert was a poet, others, an unfaithful husband.

In time, it will not be useful to ask anyone anything as no-one will be able to distinguish between fact and imagination.

If things had been different Albert could have died another way – and could have lived long enough to meet Nelson Mandela and ask him, perhaps, if freedom hung heavy after all that imprisonment – but things were not.

Monday, 12th January.

It is painful to see the mourning garden tangled with flowers and shrivelling. Even the light is different – it doesn't fall across a table or a book or through curtains in quite the same way and the moon seems to sidle under trees to light up the lawn.

'I am not going into the boring details of the aftermath of our terrible loss,' says Eve to her bridge friends, wiping a crumb of cheese scone off the corner of her mouth. 'What has happened has happened. This is clear. How to get over this is unclear.

Let me just say that it is frightening to find yourself sitting at the end of the day just as you were in the morning – doing nothing but watch the sun climb up and down the garden wall.'

The woman in the green dress (whose lipstick is like a smear of jam on her mouth and who has begun to straighten her hair so she can look like a white woman) is sure she has lost something, but not something she ever really had a hold of.

She throws herself at a rose bush, saying, 'a spirit which swept through my room one night told me to do this. Albert has gone with no thought for my feelings and without leaving any money in an envelope.'

But she says all this with the uncertain feeling of having said the wrong thing.

Because she senses that the white house is judging her, she walks away from it with the sunken air of someone whom life is pushing forwards – whether she wants it to or not.

Beauty continues to iron the tablecloths till they shine. (At the time of Albert's death, she was bent over her sewing machine, stitching a tablecloth).

She continues to drink coffee in the morning and tea in the afternoon but the news is too tragic for her to continue sprinkling her two sugars.

She feels restless and cleans Albert's room (where the bed stands empty in the middle of the floor and spots of light shine through the window), but she can't get a picture out of her mind of Albert lying in a pool of moonlight with a smile on his face and his head on the side.

She says, 'as soon as I woke the next day I felt Albert gone. I knew before anyone else because I could not smell his smell crossing me on my way to the kitchen.'

Beauty smiles too much in the face of her loss because she has work to do but she feels herself curling up like a leaf which is only vaguely involved in what the rest of the tree is doing.

She is so used to people dying she takes the death of Albert for granted but she still rubs her cleaning cloth up and down the garden bench in remembrance of him and because Albert might appear again – you never know – giving her the chance to show him how the flowers have grown.

She wants Albert back so that the familiar annoyances like unpolished silver or dirty floors can replace the more problematic questions of life and death.

(If you knew the dead well enough and listened to them closely enough when they were alive, you might be able to imagine what they would say now.

If Albert were here now, he would say, 'This is not it at all. This is not how it happened at all.')

Albert's story won't leave Beauty alone.

There will be days when she sees Albert emerge as the sun drops behind the jacarandas. There will be days when she journeys from room to room because keeping still is too exhausting. (This will go on for a while).

And there will be days when she sews until ill health gets the better of her – but her contentment from sewing keeps her company.

One day when the bridge ladies are hard at work describing their gardens and dining rooms in colour with words like 'teal', 'mouse' and 'blush pink' and Beauty is standing behind them serving tea from a tray, 'his brother-in-law did it' falls out of her mouth.

Because Beauty's voice is surprisingly deep and low, no-one hears her and no-one replies.

'Maybe the truth doesn't matter – but I would prefer to know it,' Beauty sighs.

The lady who turned purple and wood-like responds, 'I had not thought of that before.'

She had.

(The truth WILL seep out like silence from under a closed door – and be heard.

Eve will be gone by then and Beauty's family will come down to collect her, saying, 'it's time you came home.')

Albert's body is buried below a slight mound of earth with a cross made of twigs placed on top. Albert is not a white man so there is no decent burial. People bury him near a eucalyptus tree then say a prayer.

At first, his soul hovers near the tree – afraid to leave his heart, home to it for forty-three years and fearing that if it travels too far, it will never come back.

(When Albert's soul does find its way, it will be lofted up by something unseen and will leave easily – on a day the earth glows with orange light – as if it had never really arrived or put down any roots which needed pulling out).

Albert wasn't planning on dying anything like so soon and, for a long time, there will be a strong feeling that nothing has happened – that Albert is living, washing floors and telling his stories under the stars.

What no-one knows is that Albert's last thought in the still minutes before his terror died inside him, was of the time – so the last person on Albert's mind was Jack.

After that, all was replaced by indifference to the crazy world under the night sky which gave birth to a new star as the blade met Albert's skin.

Summer jumps directly to winter and the first snow for twenty years falls on the city.

No one imagined it would snow in a place so green and people say, 'this is lucky. We have a white city under white skies' and 'the goldmines glow with snow.' (The truth is that the garden is still out in summer leaf and the grass still green so this snow comes to nothing much when it reaches the ground. Shops put on feeble displays of winter wonderlands which dazzle shoppers' eyes and have to be dismantled).

The sun continues its rise and fall, shining through every ritual of daily life like someone who hasn't heard news of a disaster.

The pool stays as bright as glass, grasslands keep stretching up to the sea, rainbows dance on mirrors and the seasons change – as ever they did – bringing new memories and confirming some belief or other about time passing and life going on.

The Chinaman, who is two decades older than Albert, wonders how Albert could have stolen a march on him.

He wears his hair cut so short no-one notices it is thinning but he wonders if he should grow a beard. He keeps on wishing people 'the best game of their lives'.

He runs his nail up and down his chest and works until he makes enough money to buy his son a large maroon car and a house near the goldmines. Although the South African sun is brighter and the cars shinier, he returns to China the day Nelson Mandela emerges from the darkness (and the whole country's dreams light up – as if everyone walked out of prison with him). He leaves behind his South African wife (whose name is Sophie).

The Chinaman may have known love but can't remember saying 'I love you' to anyone.

'It may be that I am better off without love,' he sighs. 'My friendship with Albert was the last reminder that I missed out on so many things and Albert and I will never see each other again.'

He fears that the high point of his life was his visit to the drive-in cinema where the ticket clerk spoke Chinese. Although he is not sure what, he decides to do something meaningful with his life before it is too late.

He says, 'apartheid did not interfere with me but I worry that life may discard me when I grow old – or, shall I say, unemployable.'

Albert's wife never imagined Albert's death – never.

She waits in silence for him to return and is lost without his explanations. She can't get on with her ordinary life, her body is not behaving properly and she eats food she can't remember deciding to eat.

'All Albert needed to do was sit down behind a crate or tree and hide till the sun rose. There were other possibilities – surely...' she cries.

And, although she mourned Albert long before his death, she never realised how much she needed his approval.

Albert has gone for good and all she has left of him is her son.

She must carry on until her mourning becomes the past and she can live once more in the present. Her sadness will leave her only when she sees she cannot connect the reality any more with the person she loved in her head. It is up to her to go one way or the other: she might recover, fall in love with someone else or she might grow hard and solitary around her sadness.

(Within a year, she will find new love – just at the point when she thinks her heart has dried up. She will marry the man who stood near her at Albert's funeral because his wife's grave was next to Albert's. She will become rich, happy and never experience further uncertainty.

She cannot know this now).

The strange middle-aged woman will ever be bound to the wall at the bottom of the garden, watching to see what turn events take.

The sentence, 'everyone else gets everything wrong' will lurk in a corner of her mind waiting for the chance to come out.

What is Jack's opinion?

He has no opinion – except to say that he dislikes change.

The soothing lack of choice in Jack's life will mean that he will garden with his trilby on his head, taking care of bushes and creepers while listening to the voice of the presenter of 'Forces Favourites' on the radio and wondering at the mystery of trees. (When the radio programme comes to an end, Jack will have lost a close friend).

Jack is an urban person now – detached and solitary, walking the empty streets. But, inside, he is ticking away, all by himself, the same Jack who was there before any of this happened.

Jack will never leave Johannesburg, thinking that he might just guard the city by living there – as if things were that simple. He will buy a wrist watch which he angles to make sure it catches the sun.(Jack always seems to know what time it is, anyway, and is never more than five or six minutes out).

He will earn his living teaching children to tell the time by judging shadows, saying (with authority), 'sit beside me, children. Sit beside me' – taking Oscar's words for his own as if the only way he could talk properly about anything were in Oscar's language.

Jack will continue to step out with the belief that things will work out because he has the same right as any to step out and because he is more or less always in a good mood.

'All I have to do from now on is try not to die,' he will say to himself (as if to a stranger he has never met) fearing that if he dies, someone else will eat the grapes and the sun continue to shine and dragonflies fly above the swimming pool without him.

Nelson Mandela will say, 'after climbing a great hill one only finds that there are many more hills to climb.'

Nelson Mandela will also say something like, 'At first, you have to suggest there is no difference between black and white if you want to heal a nation. But then, you have to get to a point where it is more insulting to say this than to speak of the differences between people. People have to learn to live together without betraying what they really feel inside.'

(Good words – but no-one knows, for certain, whether Nelson

Mandela said all this – or not.)

Nelson Mandela, himself, will die and all the people of the world will gather together to mourn him.

Oscar will cough more. He will always be on the lookout for signs that his past was just that – but, of course, it wasn't.

Oscar will say, 'Everything matters. But, in time, all unanswered questions dissolve into dust.'

There will always be a bit of the Lithuanian accent in Oscar's speech but he will not suspect it himself and, as time goes on, it will be hardly perceptible.

There will be days when he sits behind his desk, studying people, knowing that life and death are meaningless without each other.

The part of his life which is safe will stay in his flower beds.

Oscar will continue to say, 'whatever happens in our lives, we see things not as they are but as we are. Who knows what people are going through when their pain isn't visible on their faces?'

Apartheid will disappear, the tide will shift and there will be other things to be ashamed of or afraid of. There will be old loyalties and new enemies because that's life. (Apartheid is so 'normal' people do not think it is apartheid, anyway). Whatever happens, apartheid won't stop the sun from entering peoples' dreams.

White men will continue to trade stories of close calls – robberies or high-jacking – and black men will talk of police raids.

Silence will settle into the brick work of the white house which has a look of being fixed in time. Albert's story belongs to it – something no other house in the street can claim, but there will be a sense of people's lives floating out of the house and freeing themselves of each other.

Housewives will come and go. Cooks, cleaners and gardeners will start work and leave off. Noise will clean where Albert cleaned and sleep where he slept – but Noise in name only for he will be a silent presence who leaves no trace.

The house will open its eyes in summer – surprised by new growth in the once neglected garden – and half close them against the winter cold. It will shimmer in spring's gentle light and crumble a bit in the autumn. There will be talk of wooden floors turning to stone and white walls, olive. There will be talk of other changes, but everything takes too long and costs too much.

Nothing much will happen in the neighbourhood and then, one day, the neighbourhood will be gone because people will be paying attention to other places.

Johannesburg will see violent uprisings and it will see peace but there will always be a conversation or a discovery – a birth or a death – which will require people to pay attention to the world so that a new story can be told.

The trees in the city will be the same as ever they were, giving no signs of being party to the crime, but they will grow taller – whether they are seen or not.

Albert will float on his back through all the tears shed over him and above all the trees of the world on his journey to heaven where Oscar's ancestors will raise their hands in greeting as he passes.

And really, that's all there is to this story except to say that on a particularly warm Saturday (and before everything goes wrong again) Eve will rub rouge on her cheeks and flounce down her quiet suburban street, going all the way under trees to the shop on the corner wearing a flared black skirt and humming 'Volare'. She will glow with light as if this were her last chance.

'Why NOT wear this skirt?' she will reply to her imaginary interrogator.

(Eve's skin will remain unblemished to the end. People will know she has aged only by her speckled hands).

Beauty will open her box of secrets. There are letters there she need never read again because she knows every word of them by heart but she will have forgotten about the penny whistle resting among them which Albert left with her for safekeeping.

Beauty, who could always sing in her head, will sing 'Today you will know that the Lord is coming' with the township choir – under her breath, at first – and with caution. No-one will be more surprised than she to find that all the words she refused to speak spill out in song – and that a voice, once heard, is free.

(She will still think of making curry with sultanas and bananas – like they do in Durban –and will continue to wonder if God hears anything.)

Although the little butterflies never leave the bottom of her stomach (and until her own brush with mortality), she will begin to see all of life in terms of change and possibility. (And she would be happy to know that someone was following her recipes in a kitchen of their own in the future.)

Until Albert's passing Alice had no idea what absence was like and for a while after it, she could not look up at the stars without thinking of Albert.

In ten years' time she will leave her city.

Alice will grow up to find that, although there are corners of her parents' lives she never visited, she will always carry them – not on her wings like the goose of her fairy tale, but in her heart.

She will want to turn round, sift through the many shades of green that colour her childhood and bring Albert back to her by writing about him before it is too late – or, rather, before there is no further use for him, dead or alive.

'Beginnings happen throughout a life and there are times when you think you are starting anew only to find yourself going backwards all over again,' says Oscar.